P9-AFN-000

TWFOL

Promised Land

BOOKS BY ROBERT B. PARKER

The Godwulf Manuscript
God Save the Child
Mortal Stakes
Promised Land

Promised Land

ROBERT B. PARKER

Houghton Mifflin Company Boston 1976

Library of Congress Cataloging in Publication Data
Parker, Robert B., date
Promised land.   I. Title.
PZ4.P244Pr   [PS3566.A686]   813'.5'4   76-20527
ISBN 0-395-24771-3

Printed in the United States of America

C 10 9 8 7 6 5 4 3 2 1

For Joan, David, and Daniel

1

I HAD BEEN urban-renewed right out of my office and had to move uptown. My new place was on the second floor of a two-story round turret that stuck out over the corner of Mass Ave and Boylston Street above a cigar store. The previous tenant had been a fortuneteller and I was standing in the window scraping her patchy gilt lettering off the pane with a razor blade when I saw him. He had on a pale green leisure suit and a yellow shirt with long pointed collar, open at the neck and spilling onto the lapels of the suit. He was checking the address on a scrap of paper and looking unhappily at the building.

"I've either got my first client in the new office," I said, "or the last of Madam Sosostris'."

Behind me Susan Silverman, in cut-off Levis and a blue-and-white-striped tank top, was working on the frosted glass of the office door with Windex and a paper towel. She stepped to the window and looked down.

"He doesn't look happy with the neighborhood," she said.

"If I were in a neighborhood that would make him happy, he couldn't afford me."

The man disappeared into the small door beside the tobacco store and a minute later I heard his footsteps on the stairs. He paused, then a knock. Susan opened the door. He looked uncertainly in. There were files on the floor in cardboard boxes that said FALSTAFF on them, the walls still smelled of rubber-based paint and brushes and cans of paint clustered on newspaper to the left of the door. It was hot in the office and I was wearing only a pair of paint-stained Levis and worse sneakers.

"I'm looking for a man named Spenser," he said.

"Me," I said. "Come on in." I laid the razor blade on the windowsill and came around the desk to shake his hand. I needed a client. I bet Philo Vance never painted his own office.

"This is Mrs. Silverman," I said. "She's helping me to move in. The city knocked down my old office." I was conscious of the trickle of sweat that was running down my chest as I talked. Susan smiled and said hello.

"My name is Shepard," he said. "Harvey Shepard. I need to talk."

Susan said, "I'll go out and get a sandwich. It's close to lunchtime. Want me to bring you back something?"

I shook my head. "Just grab a Coke or something. When Mr. Shepard and I are finished I'll take you to lunch somewhere good."

"We'll see," she said. "Nice to have met you, Mr. Shepard."

When she was gone, Shepard said, "Your secretary?"

"No," I said. "Just a friend."

"Hey, I wish I had a friend like that."

"Guy with your kind of threads," I said, "shouldn't have any trouble."

"Yeah, well, I'm married. And I work all the time."

There was silence. He had a high-colored square face with crisp black hair. He was a little soft around the jowls and his features seemed a bit blurred, but he was a good-looking guy. Black Irish. He seemed like a guy who was used to talking and his failure to do so now was making him uncomfortable. I primed the pump.

"Who sent you to me, Mr. Shepard?"

"Harv," he said. "Call me Harv, everyone does."

I nodded.

"I know a reporter on the New Bedford *Standard Times*. He got your name for me."

"You from New Bedford, Harv?"

"No, Hyannis."

"You're gonna run for President and you want me for an advance man."

"No." He did a weak uncertain smile. "Oh, I get it, Hyannis, hah."

"Okay," I said, "you're not going to run for President. You don't want me as an advance man. What is your plan?"

"I want you to find my wife."

"Okay."

"She's run away, I think."

"They do that sometimes."

"I want her back."

"That I can't guarantee. I'll find her. But I don't do kidnaping. If she comes back is between you and her."

"She just left. Me and three kids. Just walked out on us."

"You been to the cops?"

He nodded.

"They don't suspect, if you'll pardon the expression, foul play?"

He shook his head. "No, she packed up her things in a suitcase and left. I know Deke Slade personally and he is convinced she's run off."

"Slade a cop?"

"Yes, Barnstable police."

"Okay. A hundred a day and expenses. The expenses are going to include a motel room and a lot of meals. I don't want to commute back and forth from Boston every day."

"Whatever it costs, I'll pay. You want something up front?"

"Harv, if you do run for President I will be your advance man."

He smiled his weak smile again. I wasn't taking his mind off his troubles.

"How much you want?"

"Five hundred."

He took a long wallet from his inside coat pocket and took five hundred-dollar bills out of it and gave them to me. I couldn't see how much was left in the wallet. I folded them up and stuck them in my pants pocket and tried to look like they were joining others.

"I'll come down in the morning. You be home?"

"Yeah. I'm on Ocean Street, eighteen Ocean Street. When do you think you'll get there? I got just a ton of work to do. Jesus, what a time for her to walk out on us."

"I'll be there at nine o'clock. If you got pictures of her, get them ready, I'll have copies made. If you have any letters, phone bills, charge-card receipts, that sort of thing, dig them out, I'll want to see them. Check stubs? List of friends or family she might go to? How about another man?"

"Pam? Naw. She's not interested much in sex."

"She might be interested in love."

"I give her that, Spenser. All she could ever use."

"Well, whatever. How about the kids? Can I talk in front of them?"

"Yeah, we don't hide things. They know she took off. They're old enough anyway, the youngest is twelve."

"They have any thoughts on their mother's whereabouts?"

"I don't think so. They say they don't."

"But you're not certain?"

"It's just, I'm not sure they'd tell me. I mean I haven't talked with them lately as much as I should. I don't know for sure that they're leveling with me. Especially the girls."

"I have that feeling all the time about everybody. Don't feel bad."

"Easy for you."

"Yeah, you're right. You have anything else to tell me?"

He shook his head.

"Okay, I'll see you tomorrow at nine."

We shook hands.

"You know how to get there?"

"Yes," I said. "I know Hyannis pretty well. I'll find you."

"Will you find her, Spenser?"

"Yep."

2

WHEN SUSAN SILVERMAN came back from her Coke I was sitting at the desk with the five one-hundred-dollar bills spread out in front of me.

"Whose picture is on a one-hundred-dollar bill?" I said.

"Nelson Rockefeller."

"Wrong."

"David Rockefeller?"

"Never mind."

"Laurance Rockefeller?"

"Where would you like to go to lunch?"

"You shouldn't have shown me the money. I was ready to settle for Ugi's steak and onion subs. Now I'm thinking about Pier 4."

"Pier 4 it is. Think I'll have to change?"

"At least wipe the sweat off your chest."

"Come on, we'll go back to my place and suit up."

"When you get a client," Susan said, "you really galvanize into action, don't you?"

"Yes, ma'am. I move immediately for the nearest restaurant."

I clipped my gun on my right hip, put on my shirt and left the shirttail out to hide the gun and we left. It was a ten-minute walk to my apartment, most of it down the mall on Commonwealth Ave. When we got there, Susan took the first shower and I had a bottle of Amstel while I called for reservations. In fact I had three.

6

Pier 4 looms up on the waterfront like a kind of Colonial Stonehenge. Used brick, old beams and a Hudson River excursion boat docked alongside for cocktails. A monument to the expense account, a temple of business lunches. One of the costumed kids at the door parked my convertible with an embarrassed look. Most of the cars in the lot were newer and almost none that I could see had as much gray tape patching the upholstery.

"That young man seemed disdainful of your car," Susan said.

"One of the troubles with the culture," I said. "No respect for age."

There'd be a wait for our table. Would we care for a cocktail in the lounge? We would. We walked across the enclosed gangplank to the excursion boat and sat and looked at Boston Harbor. Susan had a Margarita, I had some Heinekens. Nobody has Amstel. Not even Pier 4.

"What does your client want you to do?"

"Find his wife."

"Does it sound difficult?"

"No. Sounds like she's simply run off. If she has she'll be easy to find. Most wives who run off don't run very far. The majority of them, in fact, want to be found and want to come home."

"That doesn't sound particularly liberated."

"It isn't particularly liberated but it's the way it is. For the first time the number of runaway wives exceeds the number of runaway husbands. They read two issues of *Ms.* magazine, see Marlo Thomas on a talk show and decide they can't go on. So they take off. Then they find out that they have no marketable skills. That ten or fifteen years of housewifing has prepared them for nothing else and they end up washing dishes or waiting table or pushing a mop and they want out. Also lots of them get lonesome."

"And they can't just go home," Susan said, "because they are embarrassed and they can't just go crawling back."

"Right. So they hang around and hope someone looks for them."

"And if someone does look for them it's a kind of communicative act. That is, the husband cared enough about them to try to find them. It's a gesture, in its odd way, of affection."

"Right again. But the guilt, particularly if they have kids, the guilt is killing them. And when they get home things are usually worse than they were when they left."

Susan sipped at her Margarita. "The husband has a new club to beat her with."

I nodded. "Yep. And partly he's right. Partly he's saying, hey, you son of a bitch. You ducked out on us. You left me and the kids in the goddamned lurch and you ran. That's no reason for pride, sweetheart. You owe us."

"But," Susan said.

"Of course, but. Always but. But she's lived her life in terms of them and she needs a chance to live it in terms of her. Natch." I shrugged and drank the rest of my beer.

"You make it sound so routine."

"It is routine in a way," I said. "I've seen it enough. In the sixties I spent most of my time looking for runaway kids. Now I spend it looking for runaway mommas. The mommas don't vary the story too much."

"You also make it sound, oh I don't know, trivial. Or, commonplace. As if you didn't care. As if they were only items in your work. Things to look for."

"I don't see much point to talking with a tremor in my voice. I care enough about them to look for them. I do it for the money too, but money's not hard to make. The thing, in my line of work at least, is not to get too wrapped up in caring. It tends to be bad for you." I gestured to the waitress for another beer. I looked at Susan's drink. She shook her head.

Across the harbor a 747 lifted improbably off the runway at Logan and swung slowly upward in a lumbering circle before heading west. L.A.? San Francisco?

"Suze," I said. "You and I ought to be on that."

"On what?"

"The plane. Heading west. Loosing the surly bonds of earth."

"I don't like flying."

"Whoops," I said. "I have trod on a toe."

"Why do you think so?"

"Tone, babe, tone of voice. Length of sentence, attitude of head. I am, remember, a trained investigator. Clues are my game. What are you mad at?"

"I don't know."

"That's a start."

"Don't make fun of me, Spenser. I don't exactly know. I'm mad at you, or at least in that area. Maybe I've read *Ms.* magazine, maybe I spend too much time seeing Marlo Thomas on talk shows. I was married and divorced and maybe I know better than you do what this man's wife might be going through."

"Maybe you do," I said. The maître d' had our table and we were silent as we followed him to it. The menus were large and done in a stylish typeface. The price of lobster was discreetly omitted.

"But say you do," I picked up. "Say you understand her problem better than I do. What's making you mad?"

She looked at her menu. "Smug," she said. "That's the word I was looking for, a kind of smugness about that woman's silly little fling."

The waitress appeared. I looked at Susan. "Escargots," she said to the waitress. "And the cold crab." I ordered assorted hot hors d'oeuvres and a steak. The waitress went away.

"I don't buy smug," I said. "Flip, maybe, but not smug."

"Condescending," Susan said.

"No," I said. "Annoyed, maybe, if you push me. But not at her, at all the silliness in the world. I'm sick of movements. I'm sick of people who think that a new system will take care of everything. I'm sick of people who put the cause ahead of the person. And I am sick of people, whatever sex, who dump the kids and run off: to work, to booze, to sex, to success. It's irresponsible."

The waitress reappeared with our first course. My platter of hot hors d'oeuvres included a clam Casino, an oyster Rockefeller, a fried shrimp, a soused shrimp and a stuffed mushroom cap.

"I'll trade you a mushroom cap for a snail," I said to Susan.

She picked a snail up in the tongs and put it on my plate. "I don't want the mushroom," she said.

"No need for a hunger strike, Suze, just because you're mad." I poked the snail out of its shell and ate it. "Last chance for the mushroom."

She shook her head. I ate the mushroom.

Susan said, "You don't know why she ran off."

"Neither of us does."

"But you assumed a feminist reason."

"I should not have. You are right."

"I'll take that soused shrimp," Susan said. I put it on her plate with my fork.

I said, "You know they're my favorite."

She said, "And I know you don't care that much for the mushroom caps."

"Bitch."

Susan smiled. "The way to a man's remorse," she said, "is through his stomach."

The smile did it, it always did it. Susan's smile was Technicolor, Cinemascope and stereophonic sound. I felt my stomach muscles tighten, like they always did when she smiled, like they always did when I really looked at her.

"Where in hell were you," I said, "twenty years ago?"

"Marrying the wrong guy," she said. She put her right hand out and ran her forefinger over the knuckles on my left hand as it lay on the tabletop. The smile stayed but it was a serious smile now. "Better late than never," she said.

The waitress came with the salad.

3

I WAS UP EARLY and on my way to Hyannis before the heavy rush-hour traffic started in Boston. Route 3 to the Cape is superhighway to the Sagamore Bridge. Twenty years ago there was no superhighway and you went to the Cape along Route 28 through the small southern Mass towns like Randolph. It was slow but it was interesting and you could look at people and front yards and brown mongrel dogs, and stop at diners and eat hamburgers that were cooked before your very eyes. Driving down Route 3 that morning the only person I saw outside a car was a guy changing a tire near a sign that said PLYMOUTH.

As I arched up over the Cape Cod Canal at the Sagamore Bridge, Route 3 became Route 6, the Mid-Cape Highway. In the center strip and along each roadside was scrub white pine, and some taller, an occasional maple tree and some small oak trees. At high points on the road you could see ocean on both sides, Buzzards Bay to the south, Cape Cod Bay to the north. In fact the whole Cape echoed with a sense of the ocean, not necessarily its sight and not always its scent or sound. Sometimes just the sense of vast space on each side of you. Of open brightness stretching a long way under the sun.

Route 132 took me into Hyannis center. The soothing excitements of scrub pine and wide sea gave way to McDonald's and Holiday Inn and prefab fence companies, shopping malls and

Sheraton Motor Inns, and a host of less likely places where you could sleep and eat and drink in surroundings indistinguishable from the ones you'd left at home. Except there'd be a fishnet on the wall. If Bartholomew Gosnold had approached the Cape from this direction he'd have kept on going.

At the airport circle, I headed east on Main Street. Hyannis is surprisingly congested and citylike as you drive into it. Main Street is lined with stores, many of them branches of Boston and New York stores. The motel I wanted was at the east end of town, a big handsome resort motel with a health club and a good restaurant of Victorian décor. A big green sign out front said DUNFEY'S. I had stayed there two months ago with Brenda Loring and had a nice time.

I was in my room and unpacked by nine-thirty. I called Shepard. He was home and waiting for me. Ocean Street is five minutes from the motel, an extension of Sea Street, profuse with weathered shingles and blue shutters. Shepard's house was no exception. A big Colonial with white cedar shingles weathered silver, and blue shutters at all the windows. It was on a slight rise of ground on the ocean side of Ocean Street. A white Caddie convertible with the top down was parked in front. A curving brick path ran up to the front door and small evergreens clustered along the foundation. The front door was blue. I rang the bell and heard it go bing-bong inside. To the left of the house was a beach, where the street curved. To the right was a high hedge concealing the neighbors' house next door. A blond teen-age girl in a very small lime green bikini answered the door. She looked maybe seventeen. I carefully did not leer at her when I said, "My name's Spenser to see Mr. Shepard."

The girl said, "Come in."

I stepped into the front hallway and she left me standing while she went to get her father. I closed the door behind me. The front hall was floored in flagstone and the walls appeared to be cedar paneling. There were doors on both sides and in the rear, and a stairway leading up. The ceilings were white and evenly rough, the kind of plaster ceiling that is sprayed on and shows no mark of human hand.

Shepard's daughter came back. I eyed her surreptitiously

behind my sunglasses. Surreptitious is not leering. She might be too young, but it was hard to tell.

"My dad's got company right now, he says can you wait a minute?"

"Sure."

She walked off and left me standing in the hall. I didn't insist on port in the drawing room, but standing in the hall seemed a bit cool. Maybe she was distraught by her mother's disappearance. She didn't look distraught. She looked sullen. Probably mad at having to answer the door. Probably going to paint her toenails when I'd interrupted. Terrific-looking thighs though. For a little kid.

Shepard appeared from the door past the stairs. With him was a tall black man with a bald head and high cheekbones. He had on a powder blue Levi-cut leisure suit and a pink silk shirt with a big collar. The shirt was unbuttoned to the waist and the chest and stomach that showed were as hard and unadorned as ebony. He took a pair of wraparound sunglasses from the breast pocket of the jacket and as he put them on, he stared at me over their rims until very slowly the lenses covered his eyes and he stared at me through them.

I looked back. "Hawk," I said.

"Spenser."

Shepard said, "You know each other?"

Hawk nodded.

I said, "Yeah."

Shepard said to Hawk, "I've asked Spenser here to see if he can find my wife, Pam."

Hawk said, "I'll bet he can. He's a real firecracker for finding things. He'll find the ass off of a thing. Ain't that right, Spenser?"

"You always been one of my heroes too, Hawk. Where you staying?"

"Ah'm over amongst de ofays at de Holiday Inn, Marse Spensah."

"We don't say ofays anymore, Hawk. We say honkies. And you don't do that Kingfish dialect any better than you used to."

"Maybe not, but you should hear me sing 'Shortnin' Bread,' babe."

"Yeah, I'll bet," I said.

Hawk turned toward Shepard. "I'll be in touch, Mr. Shepard," he said. They shook hands and Hawk left. Shepard and I watched him from the front door as he walked down toward the Caddie. His walk was graceful and easy yet there was about him an aura of taut muscle, of tight coiled potential, that made it seem as if he were about to leap.

He looked at my '68 Chevy, and looked back at me with a big grin. "Still first cabin all the way, huh, baby?"

I let that pass and Hawk slid into his Cadillac and drove away. Ostentatious.

Shepard said, "How do you know him?"

"We used to fight on the same card twenty years ago. Worked out in some of the same gyms."

"Isn't that amazing, and twenty years later you run into him here."

"Oh, I've seen him since then. Our work brings us into occasional contact."

"Really?"

"Yeah."

"You know, I could sense that you knew each other pretty well. Salesman's instinct at sizing people up, I guess. Come on in. Have a cup of coffee, or something? It's pretty early for a drink, I guess."

We went into the kitchen. Shepard said, "Instant okay?"

I said, "Sure," and Shepard set water to boiling in a red porcelain teakettle.

The kitchen was long with a divider separating the cooking area from the dining area. In the dining area was a big rough-hewn picnic table with benches on all four sides. The table was stained a driftwood color and contrasted very nicely with the blue floor and counter tops.

"So you used to be a fighter, huh?"

I nodded.

"That how your nose got broken?"

"Yep."

"And the scar under your eye, too, I'll bet."

"Yep."

"Geez, you look in good shape, bet you could still go a few rounds today, right?"

"Depends on who I went them with."

"You fight heavyweight?"

I nodded again. The coffee water boiled. Shepard spooned some Taster's Choice from a big jar into each cup. "Cream and sugar?"

"No thank you," I said.

He brought the coffee to the table and sat down across from me. I'd been hoping, maybe for a doughnut, or a muffin. I wondered if Hawk had gotten one.

"Cheers," Shepard said, and raised his cup at me.

"Harv," I said, "you got more troubles than a missing wife."

"What do you mean by that?"

"I mean I know Hawk, I know what he does. He's an enforcer, what the kids on my corner used to call a leg-breaker. He free-lances and these days he free-lances most often for King Powers."

"Now wait a minute. I hired you to find my wife. Whatever business I'm in with Hawk is my business. Not yours. I'm not paying you to nose around in my business."

"That's true," I said. "But if you are dealing with Hawk, you are dealing with pain. Hawk's a hurter. You owe Powers money?"

"I don't know a goddamned thing about Powers. Don't worry about Powers or Hawk or anybody else. I want you looking for my wife, not peeking into my books, you know?"

"Yeah, I know. But I've spent a lot of years doing my business with people like Hawk. I know how it goes. This time Hawk came and talked to you, pleasantly enough, spelled out how much you owed and how far behind you were on the vig and when you had to pay it by."

"How the hell do you know what we were talking about?"

"And at the end he told you, with a friendly enough smile, what would happen if you didn't pay. And then I came and he said goodby politely and he left."

"Spenser, are you going to talk about this anymore or are you going to get to work on what I hired you for."

"Harv. Hawk means it. Hawk is a bad man. But he keeps his word. If you owe money, pay it. If you haven't the money, tell me now, and we can work on the problem. But don't bullshit me, and don't bullshit yourself. If you're dealing with Hawk you are in way, way, far way, over your head."

"There's nothing to talk about. Now that's it. There's no more to say about it."

"You may even be in over mine," I said.

4

I HAD A SENSE, call it a hunch, that Shepard didn't want to talk about his dealings with Hawk, or King Powers or anybody else. He wanted to talk about his wife.

"Your wife's name is Pam, right?"

"Right."

"Maiden name?"

"What difference does that make?"

"She might start using it when she took off."

"Pam Neal." He spelled it.

"Folks living?"

"No."

"Siblings?"

He looked blank.

"Brothers or sisters," I said.

"No. She's an only child."

"Where'd she grow up?"

"Belfast, Maine. On the coast, near Searsport."

"I know where it is. She have friends up there she might visit?"

"No. She left there after college. Then her folks died. She hasn't been back in fifteen years, I'd bet."

"Where'd she go to college?"

"Colby."

"In Waterville?"

"Yeah."

"What year she graduate?"

"Nineteen fifty-four, both of us. College sweethearts."

"How about college friends?"

"Oh, hell, I don't know. I mean we still see a lot of people we went to school with. You think she might be visiting someone?"

"Well, if she ran off, she had to run somewhere. She ever work?"

He shook his head strongly. "No way. We got married right after graduation. I've supported her since her father stopped."

"She ever travel without you, separate vacations, that sort of thing?"

"No, Christ, she gets lost in a phone booth. I mean she's scared to travel. Anywhere we've ever gone, I've taken her."

"So if you were her, no work experience, no travel skills, no family other than this one, and you ran off, where would you go?"

He shrugged.

"She take money," I said.

"Not much. I gave her the food money and her house money on Monday and she took off Thursday, and she'd already done the food shopping. She couldn't a had more than twenty bucks."

"Okay, so we're back to where could she go. She needed help. There's not a lot you can do on twenty bucks. What friends could she have gone to?"

"Well, I mean most of her friends were my friends too. You know. I mean I know the husband and she knows the wife. I don't think she could be hiding out anywhere like that. One of the guys would tell me."

"Unmarried friend?"

"Hey, that's a problem. I don't think I know anybody who isn't married."

"Does your wife?"

"Not that I know. But, hell, I don't keep track of her every move. I mean she had some friends from college, I don't think ever married. Some of them weren't bad either."

"Could you give me their names, last known address, that sort of thing?"

"Jesus, I don't know. I'll try, but you gotta give me a little time. I don't really know too much about what she did during the day. I mean maybe she wrote to some of them, I don't know."

"Any who live around here?"

"I just don't know, Spenser. Maybe Millie might know."

"Your daughter?"

"Yeah, she's sixteen. That's old enough for them to have girl talk and stuff, I imagine. Maybe she's got something you could use. Want me to get her?"

"Yeah, and old phone bills, letters, that kind of thing, might be able to give us a clue as to where she'd go. And I'll need a picture."

"Yeah, okay. I'll get Millie first, and I'll look for that stuff while you're talking with her." He hadn't come right home and done it like I told him. Maybe I lacked leadership qualities.

Millie didn't look happy to talk with me. She sat at the table and turned her father's empty coffee cup in a continuous circle in front of her. Shepard went off to collect the phone bills and letters. Millie didn't speak.

"Any thoughts on where your mother might be, Millie?"

She shook her head.

"Does that mean you don't know or you won't say."

She shrugged and continued to turn the coffee cup carefully.

"You want her back?"

She shrugged again. When I turn on the charm they melt like butter.

"Why do you think she ran off?"

"I don't know," she said, staring at the cup. Already she was starting to pour out her heart to me.

"If you were she," I said, "would you run off?"

"I wouldn't leave my children," she said and there was some emphasis on the *my*.

"Would you leave your husband?"

"I'd leave him," she said and jerked her head toward the door her father had gone through.

"Why?"

"He's a jerk."

"What's jerky about him?"

She shrugged.

"Work too hard? Spend too much time away from the family?"

She shrugged again.

"Honey," I said. "On the corner I hang out, when you call someone a jerk you're supposed to say why, especially if it's family."

"Big deal," she said.

"It's one of the things that separate adults from children," I said.

"Who wants to be an adult?"

"I been both and adult is better than kid."

"Sure," she said.

"Who's your mother's best friend?" I said.

She shrugged again. I thought about getting up and throwing her through the window. It made me feel good for a minute, but people would probably call me a bully.

"You love your mother?"

She rolled her eyes at the ceiling and gave a sigh. "Course," she said and looked back at the circles she was making with the coffee cup. Perhaps I could throw it through the window instead.

"How do you know she's not in trouble?"

"I don't know."

"How do you know she's not kidnaped?"

"I don't know."

"Or sick someplace with no one to help her." Ah, the fertility of my imagination. Maybe she was the captive of a dark mysterious count in a castle on the English moors. Should I mention to the kid a fate worse than death?

"I don't know. I mean my father just said she ran away. Isn't he supposed to know?"

"He doesn't know. He's guessing. And he's trying to spare you in his jerky way from worse worry."

"Well, why doesn't he find out?"

"Ahhh, oh giant of brain, comes the light. What the hell do you think he's hired me for?"

"Well, why don't you find out." She had stopped turning the coffee cup.

"That's what I'm trying to do. Why don't you help? So far your contribution to her rescue is four I-don't-knows and six shrugs. Plus telling me your old man's a jerk but you don't know why."

"What if she really did run away and doesn't want to come back?"

"Then she doesn't come back. I almost never use my leg irons on women anymore."

"I don't know where she is."

"Why do you suppose she left?"

"You already asked me that."

"You didn't answer."

"My father got on her nerves."

"Like how?"

"Like, I don't know. He was always grabbing at her, you know. Patting her ass, or saying gimme a kiss when she was trying to vacuum. That kind of stuff. She didn't like it."

"They ever talk about it?"

"Not in front of me."

"What did they talk about in front of you?"

"Money. That is, my old man did. My old lady just kind of listened. My old man talks about money and business all the time. Keeps talking about making it big. Jerk."

"Your father ever mistreat your mother?"

"You mean hit her or something?"

"Whatever."

"No. He treated her like a goddamned queen, actually. That's what was driving her crazy. I mean he was all over her. It was gross. He was sucking after her all the time. You know?"

"Did she have any friends that weren't also friends of your father's?"

She frowned a little bit, and shook her head. "I don't think so. I don't know any."

"She ever go out with other men?"

"My mother?"

"It happens."

"Not my mother. No way."

"Is there anything you can think of, Millie, that would help me find your mother?"

"No, nothing. Don't you think I'd like her back. I have to do all the cooking and look out for my brother and sister and make sure the cleaning lady comes and a lot of other stuff."

"Where's your brother and sister?"

"At the beach club, the lucky stiffs. I have to stay home for you."

"For me?"

"Yeah, my father says I have to be the hostess and stuff till my mother comes home. I'm missing the races and everything."

"Life's hard sometimes," I said. She made a sulky gesture with her mouth. We were silent for a minute.

"The races go on all week," she said. "Everybody's there. All the summer kids and everybody."

"And you're missing them," I said. "That's a bitch."

"Well, it is. All my friends are there. It's the biggest time of the summer."

So young to have developed her tragic sense so highly.

Shepard came back in the room with a cardboard carton filled with letters and bills. On top was an 8½ x 11 studio photo in a gold filigree frame. "Here you go, Spenser. This is everything I could find."

"You sort through any of it?" I asked.

"Nope. That's what I hired you for. I'm a salesman, not a detective. I believe in a man doing what he does best. Right, Mill?"

Millie didn't answer. She was probably thinking about the races.

"A man's gotta believe in something," I said. "You know where I'm staying if anything comes up."

"Dunfey's, right? Hey, mention my name to the maître d' in The Last Hurrah, get you a nice table."

I said I would. Shepard walked me to the door. Millie didn't.

"You remember that. You mention my name to Paul over there. He'll really treat you good."

As I drove away I wondered what races they were running down at the beach club.

5

I ASKED at the town hall for directions to the police station. The lady at the counter in the clerk's office told me in an English accent that it was on Elm Street off Barnstable Road. She also gave me the wrong directions to Barnstable Road, but what can you expect from a foreigner. A guy in a Sunoco station straightened me out on the directions and I pulled into the parking lot across the street from the station a little before noon.

It was a square brick building with a hip roof and two small A dormers in front. There were four or five police cruisers in the lot beside the station: dark blue with white tops and white front fenders. On the side was printed BARNSTABLE POLICE. Hyannis is part of Barnstable Township. I knew that but I never did know what a township was and I never found anyone else who knew.

I entered a small front room. To the left behind a low rail sat the duty officer with switchboard and radio equipment. To the right a long bench where the plaintiffs and felons and penitents could sit in discomfort while waiting for the captain. All police stations had a captain you waited for when you came in. Didn't matter what it was.

"Deke Slade in?" I asked the cop behind the rail.

"Captain's busy right now. Can I help you?"

"Nope, I'd like to see him." I gave the cop my business card. He looked at it with no visible excitement.

"Have a seat," he said, nodding at the bench. "Captain'll be with you when he's free." It's a phrase they learn in the police academy. I sat and looked at the color prints of game birds on the walls on my side of the office.

I was very sick of looking at them when, about one-ten, a gray-haired man stuck his head through the door on my side of the railing and said, "Spenser?"

I said, "Yeah."

He jerked his head and said, "In here." The head jerk is another one they learn in the police academy. I followed the head jerk into a square shabby office. One window looked out on to the lot where the cruisers parked. And beyond that a ragged growth of lilacs. There was a green metal filing cabinet and a gray metal desk with matching swivel chair. The desk was littered with requisitions and flyers and such. A sign on one corner said CAPTAIN SLADE.

Slade nodded at the gray metal straight chair on my side of the desk. "Sit," he said. Slade matched his office. Square, uncluttered and gray. His hair was short and curly, the face square as a child's block, outdoors tan, with a gray blue sheen of heavy beard kept close shaven. He was short, maybe five-eight, and blocky, like an offensive guard from a small college. The kind of guy that should be running to fat when he got forty, but wasn't. "What'll you have," he said.

"Harv Shepard hired me to look for his wife. I figured you might be able to point me in the right direction."

"License?"

I took out my wallet, slipped out the plasticized photostat of my license and put it in front of him on the desk. His uniform blouse had short sleeves and his bare arms were folded across his chest. He looked at the license without unfolding his arms, then at me and back at the license again.

"Okay," he said.

I picked up the license, slipped it back in my wallet.

"Got a gun permit?"

I nodded, slipped that out of the wallet and laid it in front of him. He gave it the same treatment and said, "Okay."

I put that away, put the wallet away and settled back in the chair.

Slade said, "Far as I can tell she ran off. Voluntary. No foul play. Can't find any evidence that she went with someone. Took an Almeida bus to New Bedford and that's as far as we've gone. New Bedford cops got her description and all, but they got things more pressing. My guess is she'll be back in a week or so dragging her ass."

"How about another man?"

"She probably spent the night prior to her disappearance with a guy down the Silver Seas Motel. But when she got on the bus she appeared to be alone."

"What's the guy's name she was with?"

"We don't know." Slade rocked back in his chair.

"And you haven't been busting your tail looking to find out either."

"Nope. No need to. There's no crime here. If I looked into every episode of extramarital fornication around here I'd have the whole force out on condom patrol. Some babe gets sick of her husband, starts screwing around a little, then takes off. You know how often that happens?" Slade's arms were still folded.

"Yeah."

"Guy's got money, he hires somebody like you to look. The guy he hires fusses around for a week or so, runs up a big bill at the motel and the wife comes back on her own because she doesn't know what else to do. You get a week on the Cape and a nice tan, the husband gets a tax deduction, the broad starts sleeping around locally again."

"You do much marriage counseling?"

He shook his head. "Nope, I try to catch people that did crimes and put them in jail. You ever been a cop? I mean a real one, not a private license?"

"I used to be on the States," I said. "Worked out of the Suffolk County D.A.'s office."

"Why'd you quit?"

"I wanted to do more than you do."

"Social work," he said. He was disgusted.

"Any regular boyfriends you know of?"

He shrugged. "I know she slept around a little, but I don't think anybody steady."

"She been sleeping around long or has this developed lately?"

"Don't know."

I shook my head.

Slade said, "Spenser, you want to see my duty roster? You know how many bodies I got to work with here. You know what a summer weekend is like when the weather's good and the Kennedys are all out going to Mass on Sunday."

"You got any suggestions who I might talk to in town that could get my wheels turning?" I said.

"Go down the Silver Seas, talk with the bartender, Rudy. Tell him I sent you. He pays a lot of attention and the Silver Seas is where a lot of spit gets swapped. Pam Shepard hung out down there."

I got up. "Thank you, captain."

"You got questions I can answer, lemme know."

"I don't want to take up too much of your time."

"Don't be a smart-ass, Spenser. I'll do what I can. But I got a lot of things to look at and Pam Shepard's just one of them. You need help, gimme a call. If I can, I'll give you some."

"Yeah," I said. "Okay." We shook hands and I left.

It was two-fifteen when I pulled into the lot in front of the Silver Seas Motel. I was hungry and thirsty. While I took care of that I could talk to Rudy, start running up that big bar bill. Slade was probably right, but I'd give Shepard his money's worth before she showed up. If she was going to.

There's something about a bar on the Cape in the daytime. The brightness of lowland surrounded by ocean maybe makes the air-conditioned dimness of the bar more striking. Maybe there's more people there and they are vacationers rather than the unemployed. Whatever it is, the bar at the Silver Seas Motel had it. And I liked it.

On the outside, the Silver Seas Motel was two-storied, weathered shingles, with a verandah across both stories in front. It was tucked into the seaward side of Main Street in the middle of town between a hardware store and a store that sold scallop-shell ashtrays and blue pennants that said CAPE COD on them. The bar was on the right, off the lobby, at one end of the dining room. A lot of people were eating lunch and several were just drinking. Most of the people looked like college kids, cut-offs and T-shirts, sandals and halter tops. The décor in the place was surf wood and fishnet. Two oars crossed on one wall, a harpoon that was probably made in Hong Kong hung above the mirror behind the bar. The bartender was middle-aged and big-bellied. His straight black hair was streaked here and there with gray and hung shoulder length. He wore a white shirt with a black string bow tie like a riverboat gambler. The cuffs were turned neatly back in two careful folds. His hands were thick with long tapering fingers that looked manicured.

"Draft beer?" I asked.

"Schlitz," he said. He had a flat nose and dark coppery skin. American Indian? Maybe.

"I'll have one." He drew it in a tall straight glass. Very good. No steins, or schooners or tulip shapes. Just a tall glass the way the hops god had intended. He put down a paper coaster and put the beer on it, fed the check into the register, rang up the sale and put the check on the bar near me.

"What have you got for lunch," I said.

He took a menu out from under the bar and put it in front of me. I sipped the beer and read the menu. I was working on sipping. Susan Silverman had lately taken to reprimanding me for my tendency to empty the glass in two swallows and order another. The menu said linguica on a crusty roll. My heart beat faster. I'd forgotten about linguica since I'd been down here last. I ordered two. And another beer. Sip. Sip.

The juke box was playing something by Elton John. At least the box wasn't loud. They'd probably never heard of Johnny Hartman here. Rudy brought the sandwiches and looked at my half-sipped glass. I finished it — simple politeness, otherwise he'd have had to wait while I sipped — and he refilled the glass.

"You ever hear of Johnny Hartman," I said.

"Yeah. Great singer. Never copped out and started singing this shit." He nodded at the juke box.

"You Rudy," I said.

"Yeah."

"Deke Slade told me to come talk with you." I gave him a card. "I'm looking for a woman named Pam Shepard."

"I heard she was gone."

"Any idea where?" I took a large bite of the linguica sandwich. Excellent. The linguica had been split and fried and in each sandwich someone had put a fresh green pepper ring.

"How should I know?"

"You knew Johnny Hartman, and you add green peppers to your linguica sandwich."

"Yeah, well, I don't know where she went. And the cook does the sandwiches. I don't like green pepper in mine."

"Okay, so you got good taste in music and bad taste in food. Mrs. Shepard come in here much?"

"Lately, yeah. She's been in regular."

"With anyone?"

"With everyone."

"Anyone special?"

"Mostly young guys. In a dim light you might have a shot."

"Why?"

"You're too old, but you got the build. She went for the jocks and the muscle men."

"Was she in here with someone before she took off? That would have been a week ago Monday." I started on my second linguica sandwich.

"I don't keep that close a count. But it was about then. She was in here with a guy named Eddie Taylor. Shovel operator."

"They spend the night upstairs?"

"Don't know. I don't handle the desk. Just tend bar. I'd guess they did, the way she was climbing on him." A customer signaled Rudy for another stinger on the rocks. Rudy stepped down the bar, mixed the drink, poured it, rang up the price and came back to me. I finished my second sandwich while he did that. When he came back my beer glass was empty and he filled that without being asked. Well, I couldn't very well refuse, could I. Three with lunch was about right anyway.

"Where can I find Eddie Taylor?" I said.

"He's working on a job in Cotuit these days. But he normally gets off work at four and is in here by four-thirty to rinse out his mouth."

I looked at the clock behind the bar: 3:35. I could wait and sip my beer slowly. I had nothing better to do anyway. "I'll wait," I said.

"Fine with me," Rudy said. "One thing though, Eddie's sorta hard to handle. He's big and strong and thinks he's tough. And he's too young to know better yet."

"I'm big-city fuzz, Rudy. I'll dazzle him with wit and sophistication."

"Yeah, you probably will. But don't mention it was me that sicked you on to him. I don't want to have to dazzle him too."

6

It was four-twenty when Rudy said, "Hi, Eddie" to a big blond kid who came in. He was wearing work shoes and cut-off Levis and a blue tank top with red trim. He was a weightlifter: lots of tricep definition and overdeveloped pectoral muscles. And he carried himself as if he were wearing a medal. I'd have been more impressed with him if he weren't carrying a twenty-pound roll around his middle. He said to Rudy, "Hey, Kemo Sabe, howsa kid?"

Rudy nodded and without being asked put a shot of rye and a glass of draft beer on the bar in front of Eddie. Eddie popped down the shot and sipped at the beer.

"Heap good, red man," he said. "Paleface workem ass off today." He talked loudly, aware of an audience, assuming his Lone Ranger Indian dialect was funny. He turned around on the barstool, hooked his elbows over the bar and surveyed the room. "How's the quiff situation, Rudy?" he said.

"Same as always, Eddie. You don't usually seem to have any trouble." Eddie was staring across the room at two college-age girls drinking Tom Collinses. I got up and walked down the bar and slipped onto the stool beside him. I said, "You Eddie Taylor?"

"Who wants to know?" he said, still staring at the girls.

"There's a fresh line," I said.

He turned to look at me now. "Who the hell are you?"

I took a card out of my jacket pocket, handed it to him. "I'm looking for Pam Shepard," I said.

"Where'd she go?" he said.

"If I knew I'd go there and look for her. I was wondering if you could help me."

"Buzz off," he said and turned his stare back at the girls.

"I understand you spent the night with her just before she disappeared."

"Who says?"

"Me, I just said it."

"What if I did? I wouldn't be the first guy. What's it to you?"

"Poetry," I said. "Pure poetry when you talk."

"I told you once, buzz off. You hear me. You don't want to get hurt, you buzz off."

"She good in bed?"

"Yeah, she was all right. What's it to you?"

"I figure you had a lot of experience down here, and I'm new on the scene, you know? Just asking."

"Yeah, I've tagged a few around the Cape. She was all right. I mean for an old broad she had a nice tight body, you know. And, man, she was eager. I thought I was gonna have to nail her right here in the bar. Ask Rudy. Huh, Rudy? Wasn't that Shepard broad all over me the other night?"

"You say so, Eddie." Rudy was cleaning his thumbnail with a matchbook cover. "I never notice what the customers do."

"So you did spend the night with her?" I said.

"Yeah. Christ, if I hadn't she'd have dropped her pants right here in the bar."

"You already said that."

"Well, it's goddamned so, Jack, you better believe it."

Eddie dropped another shot of bar whiskey and sipped at a second beer chaser that Rudy had brought without being asked.

"Did you know her before you picked her up?"

"Hell, I didn't pick her up, she picked me up. I was just sitting here looking over the field and she came right over and sat down and started talking to me."

"Well, then, did you know her before she picked you up?"

Eddie shrugged, and gestured his shot glass at Rudy. "I'd seen her around. I didn't really know her, but I knew she was around, you know, that she was easy tail if you were looking." Eddie drank his shot as soon as Rudy poured it, and when he put the glass back on the bar Rudy filled it again.

"She been on the market long," I said. Me and Eddie were really rapping now, just a couple of good old boys, talking shop. Eddie drained his beer chaser, burped loudly, laughed at his burp. Maybe I wouldn't be able to dazzle him with my sophistication.

"On the market? Oh, you mean, yeah, I get you. No, not so long. I don't think I noticed her or heard much about her before this year. Maybe after Christmas, guy I know banged her. That's about the first I heard." His tongue was getting a little thick and his S's were getting slushy.

"Was your parting friendly?" I said.

"Huh?"

"What was it like in the morning when you woke up and said goodby to each other?"

"You're a nosy bastard," he said and looked away, staring at the two college girls across the room.

"People have said that."

"Well, I'm saying it."

"Yes, you are. And beautifully."

Eddie turned his stare at me. "What are you, a wise guy?"

"People have said that too."

"Well, I don't like wise guys."

"I sort of figured you wouldn't."

"So get lost or I'll knock you on your ass."

"And I sort of figured you'd put it just that way."

"You looking for trouble, Jack, I'm just the man to give it to you."

"I got all the trouble I need," I said. "What I'm looking for is information. What kind of mood was Pam Shepard in the morning after she'd been all over you?"

Eddie got off the barstool and stood in front of me. "I'm telling you for the last time. Get lost or get hurt." Rudy started drifting toward the phone. I checked the amount of room in front of the bar. Maybe ten feet. Enough. I said to Rudy, "It's okay. No one will get hurt. I'm just going to show him something."

I stood up. "Tubbo," I said to Eddie, "if you make me, I can put you in the hospital, and I will. But you probably don't believe me, so I'll have to prove it. Go ahead. Take your shot."

He took it, a right-hand punch that missed my head when I moved. He followed up with a left that missed by about the same margin when I moved the other way.

"You'll last about two minutes doing that," I said. He rushed at me and I rolled around him. "Meanwhile," I said, "if I wanted to I could be hitting you here." I tapped him open-handed on the right cheek very fast three times. He swung again and I stepped a little inside the punch and caught it on my left forearm. I caught the second one on my right. "Or here," I said and patted him rat-a-tat with both hands on each cheek. The way a grandma pats a child. I stepped back away from him. He was already starting to breathe hard. "Some shape you're in, kid. In another minute you won't be able to get your arms up."

"Back off, Eddie," Rudy said from behind the bar. "He's a pro, for crissake, he'll kill you if you keep shoving him."

"I'll shove the son of a bitch," Eddie said and made a grab at me. I moved a step to my right and put a left hook into his stomach. Hard. His breath came out in a hoarse grunt and he sat down suddenly. His face blank, the wind knocked out of him, fighting to get his breath. "Or there," I said.

Eddie got his breath partially back and climbed to his feet. Without looking at anyone he headed, wobbly legged, for the men's room. Rudy said to me, "You got some good punch there."

"It's because my heart is pure," I said.

"I hope he don't puke all over the floor in there," Rudy said.

The other people in the room, quiet while the trouble had flared, began to talk again. The two college girls got up and left, their drinks unfinished, their mothers' parting fears confirmed. Eddie came back from the men's room, his face pale and wet where he'd probably splashed it with water.

"The boilermakers will do it to you," I said. "Slow you down and tear up your stomach."

"I know guys could take you," Eddie said. There was no starch in his voice when he said it, and he didn't look at me.

"I do too," I said. "And I know guys who can take them. After a while counting doesn't make much sense. You just got into something I know more about than you do."

Eddie hiccupped.

"Tell me about how you left each other in the morning," I said. We were sitting at the bar again.

"What if I don't?" Eddie was looking at the small area of bar top encircled by his forearms.

"Then you don't. I don't plan to keep punching you in the stomach."

"We woke up in the morning and I wanted to go one more time, you know, sort of a farewell pop, and she wouldn't let me touch her. Called me a pig. Said if I touched her she'd kill me. Said I made her sick. That wasn't what she said before. We were screwing our brains out half the night and next morning she calls me a pig. Well, I don't need that shit, you know? So I belted her and walked out. Last I seen her she was lying on her back on the bed crying loud as a bastard. Just staring up at the ceiling and screaming crying." He shook his head. "What a weird bitch," he said. "I mean five hours before she was screwing her brains out for me."

I said, "Thanks, Eddie." I took a twenty-dollar bill out of my wallet and put it on the bar. "Take his out too, Rudy, and keep what's left."

When I left, Eddie was still looking at the bar top inside his forearms.

7

I HAD LAMB STEW and a bottle of Burgundy for supper and then headed into my room to start on the box of bills and letters Shepard had given me. I went through the personal mail first and found it sparse and unenlightening. Most people throw away personal mail that would be enlightening, I'd found. I got all the phone bills together and made a list of the phone numbers and charted them for frequency. Then I cross-charted them for locations. A real sleuth, sitting on the motel bed in my shorts shuffling names and numbers. There were three calls in the past month to a number in New Bedford, the rest were local. I assembled all the gasoline credit-card receipts. She had bought gasoline twice that month in New Bedford. The rest were around home. I catalogued the other credit-card receipts. There were three charges from a New Bedford restaurant. All for more than thirty dollars. The other charges were local. It was almost midnight when I got through all of the papers. I made a note of the phone number called in New Bedford, of the New Bedford restaurant and the name of the gas station in New Bedford, then I stuffed all the paper back in the carton, put the carton in the closet and went to bed. I spent most of the night dreaming about phone bills and charge receipts and woke up in the morning feeling like Bartleby the Scrivener.

I had room service bring me coffee and corn muffins and at nine-o-five put in a call to the telephone business office in New Bedford. A service rep answered.

"Hi," I said, "Ed MacIntyre at the Back Bay business office in Boston. I need a listing for telephone number 334-3688, please."

"Yes, Mr. MacIntyre, one moment please . . . that listing is Alexander, Rose. Three Centre Street, in New Bedford."

I complimented her on the speed with which she found the listing, implied perhaps a word dropped to the district manager down there, said goodby with smily pleasant overtones in my voice and hung up. Flawless.

I showered and shaved and got dressed. Six hours of paper shuffling had led me to a surmise that the Hyannis cops had begun by checking the bus terminal. She was in New Bedford. But I had an address, maybe not for her, but for someone. It pays to do business with your local gumshoe. Personalized service.

The drive to New Bedford up Route 6 was forty-five miles and took about an hour through small towns like Wareham and Onset, Marion and Mattapoisett. Over the bridge from Fairhaven across the interflow of the harbor and the Acushnet River, New Bedford rose steeply from the docks. Or what was left of it. The hillside from the bridge to the crest looked like newsreel footage of the Warsaw ghetto. Much of the center of the city had been demolished and urban renewal was in full cry. Purchase Street, one of the main streets the last time I'd been in New Bedford, was now a pedestrian mall. I drove around aimlessly in the bulldozed wasteland for perhaps ten minutes before I pulled off into a rutted parking area and stopped. I got out, opened the trunk of my car and got out a street directory for Massachusetts.

Centre Street was down back of the Whaling Museum. I knew where the Whaling Museum was. I got back in the car, drove up the hill and turned left past the public library. Out front they still had the heroic statue of the harpooner in the whaleboat. A dead whale or a stove boat. The choices then were simple, if drastic. I turned left down the hill toward the water, then onto Johnny Cake Hill and parked near the Whaling Museum, in front of the Seaman's Bethel.

I checked my street map again and walked around the Whaling Museum to the street behind it and looked and there was Centre Street. It was a short street, no more than four or five buildings long, and it ran from North Water Street, behind the museum, to Front Street, which paralleled the water. It was an old street, weedy and dank. Number three was a narrow two-story building with siding of gray asbestos shingles and a crumbly looking red brick chimney in the center of the roof. The roof shingles were old and dappled in various shades as though someone had patched it periodically with what he had at hand. It needed more patching. There was worn green paint on the trim here and there and the front door on the right side of the building face was painted red. It had the quality of an old whore wearing lipstick.

I hoped she wasn't in there. I wanted to find her but I hated to think of her coming from the big sunny house in Hyannis to burrow in rat's alley. What to do now? No one knew me, neither Rose Alexander or Pam Shepard, nor, as far as I knew, anyone in New Bedford. In fact the number of places where I could go and remain anonymous continuously amazed me. I could enter on any pretext and look around. Or I could stake it out and wait and watch and see what happened. Or I could knock on the door and ask for Pam Shepard. The safest thing was to stand around and watch. I liked to know as much as I could before I went in where I hadn't been before. That would take time, but I wouldn't run the risk of scaring anyone off. I looked at my watch: 12:15. I went back up toward what was left of the business district and found a restaurant. I had fried clams and cole slaw and two bottles of beer. Then I strolled back down to Centre Street and took up station about five past one. On North Water Street a municipal crew was at work with a backhoe and some jackhammers, while several guys with shirts and ties and yellow hard hats walked around with clipboards and conferred. Nobody came down Centre Street, or up it. Nobody had anything to do with Centre Street. No evidence of life appeared at number three. I had picked up a copy of the New Bedford *Standard Times* on my way back from lunch and I read it while I leaned on a telephone pole on the corner of North Water and Centre. I read everything, glancing regularly over the rim of the paper to check the house. I read about a bean supper at the Congregational church in Mattapoisett, about a father-son baseball game at the junior high school field in Rochester, about a local debutante's ball at the Wamsutta Club. I read the horoscope, the obituaries, the editorial, which took a strong stand against the incursion of

Russian trawlers into local waters. I read "Dondi" and hated it. When I finished the paper, I folded it up, walked the short length of Centre Street and leaned against the doorway of an apparently empty warehouse on the corner of Centre and Front streets.

At three o'clock a wino in a gray suit, a khaki shirt and an orange flowered tie stumbled into my doorway and urinated in the other corner. When he got through I offered to brush him off and hand him a towel but he paid me no attention and stumbled off. What is your occupation, sir? I'm an outdoor men's room attendant. I wondered if anyone had ever whizzed on Allan Pinkerton's shoe.

At four-fifteen Pam Shepard came out of the shabby house with another woman. Pam was slim and Radcliffy looking with a good tan and her brown hair back in a tight French twist. She was wearing a chino pantsuit that displayed a fine-looking backside. I'd have to get closer but she looked worth finding. The woman she was with was smaller and sturdier looking. Short black hair, tan corduroy jeans and a pink muslin shirt like Indira Gandhi. They headed up the street toward the museum and I swung along behind. We went up the hill, past the museum and turned left on the Purchase Street pedestrian mall. The mall had been created by curbing across the intersection streets and had a homemade look to it. Pam Shepard and her friend went into a supermarket and I stood under the awning of a pawnshop across the street and watched them through the plate-glass window. They bought some groceries, consulting a shopping list as they went, and in about a half-hour they were back out on the street, each with a large brown paper sack in her arms. I followed them back to the house on Centre Street and watched them disappear inside. Well, at least I knew where she was. I resumed my telephone pole. The warehouse door had lost some of its appeal.

It got dark and nothing else happened. I was beginning to hope for the wino again. I was also hungry enough to eat at a Hot Shoppe. I had some thinking it over to do and while I always did that better eating, the fried clams had not sold me on New Bedford cuisine and I would probably have to sleep sometime later on anyway. So I went back and got my car and headed back for Hyannis. There was a parking ticket under the wiper but it blew off somewhere near a bowling alley in Mattapoisett.

During the ride back to Hyannis I decided that the best move would be to go back to New Bedford in the morning and talk with Pam Shepard. In a sense I'd done what I hired on for. That is, I had her located and could report that she was alive and under no duress. It should be up to Shepard to go and get her. But it didn't go down right, giving him the address and going back to Boston. I kept thinking of Eddie Taylor's final look at her, lying on the bed on her back screaming at the ceiling. There had been a pathetic overdressed quality to her as she came out of the shabby two-story on Centre Street. She'd had on pendant earrings.

It was nine-thirty when I got back to the motel. The dining room was still open so I went in and had six oysters and a half bottle of Chablis and a one-pound steak with Béarnaise sauce and a liter of beer. The salad had an excellent house dressing and the whole procedure was a great deal more pleasant than hanging around in a doorway with an incontinent wino. After dinner I went back to my room and caught the last three innings of the Sox game on channel six.

8

IN THE MORNING I was up and away to New Bedford before eight. I stopped at a Dunkin Donuts shop for a training-table breakfast to go, and ate my doughnuts and drank my coffee as I headed up the Cape with the sun at my back. I hit New Bedford at commuter time and while it wasn't that big a city its street system was so confused that the traffic jam backed up across the bridge into Fairhaven. It was nine-forty when I got out of the car and headed for the incongruous front door at 3 Centre Street. There was no doorbell and no knocker so I rapped on the red panels with my knuckles. Not too hard, the door might fold.

A big, strong-looking young woman with light brown hair in a long single braid opened the door. She had on Levis and what looked like a black leotard top. She was obviously braless, and, less noticeably, shoeless.

"Good morning," I said, "I'd like to speak with Pam Shepard, please."

"I'm sorry, there's no Pam Shepard here."

"Will she be back soon?" I was giving her my most engaging smile. Boyish. Open. Mr. Warm.

"I don't know any such person," she said.

"Do you live here?" I said.

"Yes."

"Are you Rose Alexander?"

"No." Once I give them the engaging smile they just slobber all over me.

"Is she in?"

"Who are you?"

"I asked you first," I said.

Her face closed down and she started to shut the door. I put my hand flat against it and held it open. She shoved harder and I held it open harder. She seemed determined.

"Madam," I said. "If you will stop shoving that door at me, I will speak the truth to you. Even though, I do not believe you have spoken the truth to me."

She paid no attention. She was a big woman and it was getting hard to hold the door open effortlessly.

"I stood outside this house most of yesterday and saw Pam Shepard and another woman come out, go shopping and return with groceries. The phone here is listed to Rose Alexander." My shoulder was beginning to ache. "I will talk civilly with Pam Shepard and I won't drag her back to her husband."

Behind the young woman a voice said, "What the hell is going on here, Jane?"

Jane made no reply. She kept shoving at the door. The smaller, black-haired woman I'd seen with Pam Shepard yesterday appeared. I said, "Rose Alexander?" She nodded. "I need to talk with Pam Shepard," I said.

"I don't . . . ." Rose Alexander started.

"You do too," I said. "I'm a detective and I know such things. If you'll get your Amazon to unhand the door we can talk this all out very pleasantly."

Rose Alexander put her hand on Jane's arm. "You'd better let him in, Jane," she said gently. Jane stepped away from the door and glared at me. There were two bright smudges of color on her cheekbones, but no other sign of exertion. I stepped into the hall. My shoulder felt quite numb as I took my hand off the door. I wanted to rub it but was too proud. What price machismo?

"May I see some identification?" Rose Alexander said.

"Certainly." I took the plastic-coated photostat of my license out of my wallet and showed it to her.

"You're not with the police then," she said.

"No, I am self-employed," I said.

"Why do you wish to talk with me?"

"I don't," I said. "I wish to talk with Pam Shepard."

"Why do you wish to talk with her?"

"Her husband hired me to find her."

"And what were you to do when you did?"

"He didn't say. But he wants her back."

"And you intend to take her?"

"No, I intend to talk with her. Establish that she's well and under no duress, explain to her how her husband feels and see if she'd like to return."

"And if she would not like to return?"

"I won't force her."

Jane said, "That's for sure," and glared at me.

"Does her husband know she's here?" Rose Alexander asked.

"No."

"Because you've not told him?"

"That's right."

"Why?"

"I don't know. I guess I just wanted to see what was happening in the china shop before I brought in the bull."

"I don't trust you," Rose Alexander said. "What do you think, Jane?"

Jane shook her head.

"I'm not here with her husband, am I?"

"But we don't know how close he is," Rose Alexander said.

"Or who's with him," Jane said.

"Who's with him?" I was getting confused.

Rose said, "You wouldn't be the first man to take a woman by force and never doubt your right."

"Oh," I said.

"We back down from you now," Jane said, "and it will be easier next time. So we'll draw the line here, up front, first time."

"But if you do," I said, "you'll make me use force. Not to take anyone, but to see that she's in fact okay."

"You saw that yesterday," Jane said. The color was higher on her cheekbones now, and more intense. "You told me you saw Pam and Rose go shopping together."

"I don't think you've got her chained in the attic," I said. "But duress includes managing the truth. If she has no chance to hear me and reject me for herself she's not free, she's under a kind of duress."

"Don't you try to force your way in," Jane said. "You'll regret it, I promise you." She had stepped back away from me and shifted into a martial arts stance, her feet balanced at right angles to each other in a kind of T stance, her open hands held in front of her in another kind of T, the left hand vertical, the right horizontal above it. She looked like she was calling for time out. Her lips were pulled back and her breath made a hissing sound as it squeezed out between her teeth.

"You had lessons?" I asked.

Rose Alexander said, "Jane is very advanced in karate. Do not treat her lightly. I don't wish to hurt you, but you must leave." Her black eyes were quite wide and bright as she spoke. Her round pleasant face was flushed. I didn't believe the part about not wishing to hurt me.

"Well, I'm between a rock and a hard place right now. I don't want you to hurt me either, and I don't take Jane lightly. On the other hand the more you don't want me to see Pam Shepard, the more I think I ought to. I could probably go for the cops, but by the time we got back, Pam Shepard would be gone. I guess I'm going to have to insist."

Jane kicked me in the balls. Groin just doesn't say it. I'd never fought with a woman before and I wasn't ready. It felt like it always does: nausea, weakness, pain and an irresistible compulsion to double over. I did double over. Jane chopped down on the back of my neck. I twisted away and the blow landed on the big trapezius muscles without doing any serious damage. I straightened up. It hurt but not as much as it was going to if I didn't make a comeback. Jane aimed the heel of her hand at the tip of my nose. I banged her hand aside with my right forearm and hit her as hard a left hook as I've used lately, on the side of her face, near the hinge of her jaw. She went over backward and lay on the floor without motion. I'd never hit a woman before and it scared me a little. Had I hit her too hard? She was a big woman but I must have outweighed her by forty pounds. Rose Alexander dropped to her knees beside Jane, and having got there didn't know what to do. I got down too, painfully, and felt her pulse. It was nice and strong and her chest heaved and fell steadily. "She's okay," I said. "Probably better than I am."

At the far end of the hall was a raised panel door that had been painted black. It opened and Pam Shepard came through it. There were tears running down her face. "It's me," she said. "It's my fault, they were just trying to protect me. If you've hurt her it's my fault."

Jane opened her eyes and stared up blankly at us. She moved her head. Rose Alexander said, "Jane?"

I said, "She's going to be all right, Mrs. Shepard. You didn't make her kick me in the groin."

She too got down on the floor beside Jane. I got out of the way and leaned on the door jamb with my arms folded, trying to get the sick feeling to go away, and trying not to show it. People did not seem to be warming to me down here. I hoped Jane and Eddie never got together.

Jane was on her feet, Pam Shepard holding one arm and Rose Alexander the other. They went down the hall toward the black door. I followed along. Through the door was a big kitchen. A big old curvy-legged gas stove on one wall, a big oilcloth-covered table in the middle of the room, a couch with a brown corduroy spread along another wall. There was a pantry at the right rear and the walls were wainscoted in narrow deal boards that reminded me of my grandmother's house. They sat Jane down in a black leather upholstered rocker. Rose went to the pantry and returned with a wet cloth. She washed Jane's face while Pam Shepard squeezed Jane's hand. "I'm all right," Jane said and pushed the wet cloth away. "How the hell did you do that," she said to me. "That kick was supposed to finish you right there."

"I am a professional thug," I said.

"It shouldn't matter," she said, frowning in puzzlement. "A kick in the groin is a kick in the groin."

"Ever do it for real before?"

"I've put in hours on the mat."

"No, not instruction. Fighting. For real."

"No," she said. "But I wasn't scared. I did it right."

"Yeah, you did, but you got the wrong guy. One of the things that a kick in the groin will do is scare the kickee. Aside from the pain and all, it's not something he's used to and he cares about the area and he tends to double over and freeze. But I've been kicked before and I know that it hurts but it's not fatal. Not even to my sex life. And so I can force myself through the pain."

"But . . ." She shook her head.

"I know," I said. "You thought you had a weapon that made you impregnable. That would keep people from shoving you around and the first time you use it you get cold-cocked. It is a good weapon, but you were overmatched. I weigh one-ninety-five, I can bench-press three hundred pounds. I used to be a fighter. And I scuffle for a living. The karate will still work for you. But you gotta remember it's not a sport in the street."

"You think, goddamn you, you think it's because you're a man . . ."

"Nope. It's because a good big person will beat a good small person every time. Most men aren't as good as I am. A lot of them aren't as good as you are."

They were all looking at me and I felt isolated, unwelcome and uneasy. I wished there were another guy there. I said to Pam Shepard, "Can we talk?"

Rose Alexander said, "You don't have to say a word to him, Pam."

Jane said, "There's no point in it, Pam. You know how you feel."

I looked at Pam Shepard. She had sucked in both lips so they were not visible, and her mouth was a thin line. She looked back at me and we held the pose for about thirty seconds.

"Twenty-two years," I said. "And you knew him before you got married. More than twenty-two years you've known Harvey Shepard. Doesn't that earn him five minutes of talk. Even if you don't like him? Even simple duration eventually obliges you."

She nodded her head, to herself, I think, more than to me. "Tell him about obligation, I've known him since nineteen fifty," she said.

I shrugged. "He's forking out a hundred dollars a day and expenses to find you."

"That's his style, the big gesture. 'See how much I love you,' but is he looking? No, you're looking."

"Better than no one looking."

"Is it?" There was color on her cheekbones now. "Is it really? Why isn't it worse? Why isn't it intrusive? Why isn't it a big pain in the ass? Why don't you all just leave me the goddamned hell alone?"

"I'm guessing," I said, "but I think it's because he loves you."

"Loves me, what the hell has that got to do with anything. He probably does love me. I never doubted that he did. So what. Does that mean I have to love him? His way? By his definition?"

Rose Alexander said, "It's an argument men have used since the Middle Ages to keep women in subjugation."

"Was that a master-slave relationship Jane was trying to establish with me?" I said.

"You may joke all you wish," Rose said, "but it is perfectly clear that men have used love as a way of obligating women. You even used the term yourself." Rose was apparently the theoretician of the group.

"Rosie," I said, "I am not here to argue sexism with you. It exists and I'm against it. But what we've got here is not a theory, it's a man and woman who've known each other a long time and conspired to produce children. I want to talk with her about that."

"You cannot," Rose said, "separate the theory from its application. And" — her look was very forceful — "you cannot get the advantage of me by using the diminutive of my name. I'm quite aware of your tricks."

"Take a walk with me," I said to Pam Shepard.

"Don't do it, Pam," Jane said.

"You'll not take her from this house," Rose said.

I ignored them and looked at Pam Shepard. "A walk," I said, "down toward the bridge. We can stand and look at the water and talk and then we'll walk back."

She nodded. "Yes," she said, "I'll walk with you. Maybe you can make him understand."

9

PROTESTS, EXCURSION and alarums followed Pam Shepard's decision but in the end it was agreed that we would, in fact, stroll
down toward the harbor and that Jane and Rose would follow
along, at a discreet distance in case I tried to chloroform her and
stuff her in a sack.

As we walked along Front Street the light was strong on her
face and I realized she was probably around my age. There were
faint lines of adulthood at her eyes and the corners of her mouth.
They didn't detract, in fact they added a little, I thought, to her
appeal. She didn't look like someone who'd need to pick up
overweight shovel operators in bars. Hell, she could have her
choice of sophisticated private eyes. I wondered if she'd object to
the urine stain on my shoe.

We turned onto the bridge and walked far enough out on it to
look at the water. The water made the city look good. Oil slick,
cigarette wrappers, dead fish, gelatinous-looking pieces of water-
soaked driftwood, an unraveled condom looking like an eel skin
against the coffee-colored water. Had it looked like this when
Melville shipped out on a whaler 130 years ago? Christ, I hope
not.

"What did you say your name was?" Pam Shepard asked.

"Spenser," I said. We leaned our forearms on the railing and
stared out toward the transmitter tower on one of the harbor
islands. The wind off the ocean was very pleasant despite the
condition of the water.

"What do you want to talk about?" Today she had on a dark blue polo shirt, white shorts and white Tretorn tennis shoes. Her legs were tan and smooth.

"Mrs. Shepard, I've found you and I don't know what to do about it. You are clearly here by choice, and you don't seem to want to go home. I hired on to find you, and if I call your husband and tell him where you are I'll have earned my pay. But then he'll come up here and ask you to come home, and you'll say no, and he'll make a fuss, and Jane will kick him in the vas deferens, and unless that permanently discourages him, and it is discouraging, you'll have to move."

"So don't tell him."

"But he's hired me. I owe him something."

"I can't hire you," she said. "I have no money."

Jane and Rose stood alertly across the roadway on the other side of the bridge and watched my every move. *Semper paratus.*

"I don't want you to hire me. I'm not trying to hold you up. I'm trying to get a sense of what I should do."

"Isn't that your problem?" Her elbows were resting on the railing and her hands were clasped. The diamond–wedding ring combination on her left hand caught the sun and glinted.

"Yes it is," I said, "but I can't solve it until I know who and what I'm dealing with. I have a sense of your husband. I need to get a sense of you."

"For someone like you, I'd think the *sanctity of marriage* would be all you'd need. A woman who runs out on her family deserves no sympathy. She's lucky her husband will take her back." I noticed the knuckles of her clasped hands were whitening a little.

"Sanctity of marriage is an abstraction, Mrs. Shepard. I don't deal in those. I deal in what it is fashionable to call people. Bodies. Your basic human being. I don't give a goddamn about the sanctity of marriage. But I occasionally worry about whether people are happy."

"Isn't happiness itself an abstraction?"

"Nope. It's a feeling. Feelings are real. They are hard to talk about so people sometimes pretend they're abstractions, or they pretend that ideas, which are easy to talk about, are more important."

"Is the equality of men and women an abstraction?"

"I think so."

She looked at me a little scornfully. "Yet the failure of that equality makes a great many people unhappy."

"Yeah. So let's work on the unhappiness. I don't know what in hell equality means. I don't know what it means in the Declaration of Independence. What's making you unhappy with your husband?"

She sighed in a deep breath and heaved it out quickly. "Oh, God," she said. "Where to begin." She stared at the transmitter tower. I waited. Cars went by behind us.

"He love you?"

She looked at me with more than scorn. I thought for a minute she was going to spit. "Yes," she said. "He loves me. It's as if that were the only basis for a relationship. 'I love you. I love you. Do you love me? Love. Love.' Shit!"

"It's better than I hate you. Do you hate me?" I said.

"Oh, don't be so goddamned superficial," she said. "A relationship can't function on one emotion. Love or hate. He's like a . . ." She fumbled for an appropriate comparison. "He's like when one of the kids eats cotton candy at a carnival on a hot day and it gets all over her and then all over you and you're sticky and sweaty and the day's been a long one, and horrible, and the kids are whiny. If you don't get away by yourself and take a shower you'll just start screaming. You have any children, Mr. Spenser?"

"No."

"Then maybe you don't know. Are you married?"

"No."

"Then certainly you don't know."

I was silent.

"Every time I walk by him he wants to hug me. Or he gives me a pat on the ass. Every minute of every day that I am with him I feel the pressure of his love and him wanting a response until I want to kick him."

"Old Jane would probably help you," I said.

"She was protecting me," Pam Shepard said.

"I know," I said. "Do you love him?"

"Harvey? Not, probably, by his terms. But in mine. Or at least

I did. Until he wore me down. At first it was one of his appeals that he loved me so totally. I liked that. I liked the certainty. But the pressure of that . . ." She shook her head.

I nodded at her encouragingly. Me and Carl Rogers.

"In bed," she said. "If I didn't have multiple orgasms I felt I was letting him down."

"Have many," I said.

"No."

"And you're worried about being frigid."

She nodded.

"I don't know what that means either," I said.

"It's a term men invented," she said. "The sexual model, like everything else, has always been male."

"Don't start quoting Rose at me," I said. "That may or may not be true, but it doesn't do a hell of a lot for our problem at the moment."

"You have a problem," Pam Shepard said. "I do not."

"Yes you do," I said. "I've been talking with Eddie Taylor."

She looked blank.

"Eddie Taylor," I said, "big blond kid, runs a power shovel. Fat around the middle, and a loud mouth."

She nodded and continued to as I described him, the lines at the corners of her mouth deepening. "And why is he a problem?"

"He isn't. But unless he made it all up, and he's not bright enough to make it up, you're not as comfortably in charge of your own destiny as you seem to be."

"I'll bet he couldn't wait to tell you every detail. Probably embellished a great deal."

"No. As a matter of fact he was quite reluctant. I had to strike him in the solar plexus."

She made a slight smiling motion with her mouth for a moment. "I must say you don't talk the way I'd have expected."

"I read a lot," I said.

"So what is my problem?"

"I don't read that much," I said. "I assume you are insecure about your sexuality and ambivalent about it. But that doesn't really mean anything that either one of us can bite into."

"Well, don't we have all the psychological jargon down pat. If my husband slept around would you assume he was insecure and ambivalent?"

"I might," I said. "Especially if he had a paroxysm the morning after and was last seen crying on the bed."

Her face got a little pink for a moment. "He was revolting. You've seen him. How I could have, with a pig like that. A drunken, foul, sweaty animal. To let him use me like that." She shivered. Across the street Jane and Rose stood poised, eyes fixed upon us, ready to spring. I felt like a cobra at a mongoose festival. "He didn't give a damn about me. Didn't care about how I felt. About what I wanted. About sharing pleasure. He just wanted to rut like a hog and when it was over roll off and go to sleep."

"He didn't strike me too much as the Continental type," I said.

"It's not funny."

"No, it isn't, no more than everything else. Laughing is better than crying though. When you can."

"Well, isn't that just so folksy and down home," she said. "What the hell do you know about laughing and crying?"

"I observe it a lot," I said. "But what I know isn't an issue. If Eddie Taylor was so revolting, why did you pick him up?"

"Because I goddamned well felt like it. Because I felt like going out and getting laid without complications. Just a simple straightforward screw without a lot of lovey-dovey — did-you-like-that–do-you-love-me crap."

"You do that much?"

"Yes. When I felt like it, and I've been feeling like it a lot these last few years."

"You usually enjoy it more than you did with old Eddie?"

"Of course, I — oh hell, I don't know. It's very nice sometimes when it happens, but afterwards I'm still hung up on guilt. I can't get over all those years of nice-girls-don't-do-it, I guess."

"A guy told me you always went for the big young jocko types. Muscle and youth."

"You have yourself in mind? You're not all that young."

"I would love to go to bed with you. You are an excellent-looking person. But I'm still trying to talk about you."

"I'm sorry," she said. "That was flirtatious, and I'm trying to change. Sometimes it's hard after a long time of being something else. Flirtatious was practically the only basis for male-female relationship through much of my life."

"I know," I said. "But what about the guy who says you go for jockos. He right?"

She was silent a while. An old Plymouth convertible went by with the top down and radio up loud. I heard a fragment of Roberta Flack as the sound dopplered past.

"I guess I do. I never really gave it much thought but I guess the kind of guy I seek out is big and young and strong looking. Maybe I'm hoping for some kind of rejuvenation."

"And a nice uncomplicated screw."

"That too."

"But not with someone who just wants to rut and roll off."

She frowned. "Oh, don't split hairs with me. You know what I mean."

"No," I said. "I don't know what you mean. And I don't think you know what you mean. I'm not trying to chop logic with you. I'm trying to find out how your head is. And I think it's a mare's nest."

"What's a mare's nest?"

"Something confused."

"Well, I'm not a mare's nest. I know what I want and what I don't want."

"Yeah? What?"

"What do you mean what?"

"I mean what do you want and what do you not want."

"I don't want to live the way I have been for twenty years."

"And what do you want?"

"Something different."

"Such as?"

"Oh" — tears showed in her eyes — "I don't know. Goddamn-it, leave me alone. How the hell do I know what I want. I want you to leave me the goddamned hell alone." The tears were on her cheeks now, and her voice had thickened. Across the bridge Rose and Jane were in animated conference. I had the feeling Jane was to be unleashed in a moment. I took out one of my cards and gave it to her.

"Here," I said. "If you need me, call me. You got any money?"

She shook her head. I took ten of her husband's ten-dollar bills out of my wallet and gave them to her. The wallet was quite thin without them.

"I won't tell him where you are," I said, and walked off the bridge and back up the hill toward my car back of the museum.

10

HARVEY SHEPARD had a large purple bruise under his right eye and it seemed to hurt him when he frowned. But he frowned anyway. "Goddamnit," he said. "I laid out five hundred bucks for that information and you sit there and tell me I can't have it. What kind of a goddamned business is that?"

"I'll refund your advance if you want, but I won't tell you where she is. She's well, and voluntarily absent. I think she's confused and unhappy but she's safe enough."

"How do I know you've even seen her. How do I know you're not trying to rip me off for five bills and expenses without even looking for her?"

"Because I offered to give it back," I said.

"Yeah, lots of people offer but try to get the money."

"She was wearing a blue polo shirt, white shorts, white Tretorn tennis shoes. Recognize the clothes?"

He shrugged.

"How'd you get the mouse?" I said.

"The what?"

"The bruise on your face. How'd you get it?"

"For crissake, don't change the subject. You owe me information and I want it. I'll take you right the hell into court if I have to."

"Hawk lay that on you?"

"Lay what?"

"The mouse. Hawk give it to you?"

"You keep your nose out of my business, Spenser. I hired you to find my wife, and you won't even do that. Never mind about Hawk."

We were in his office on the second floor overlooking Main Street. He was behind his big Danish modern desk. I was in the white leather director's chair. I got up and walked to the door.

"Come here," I said. "I want you to see something in the outer office."

"What the hell is out there?"

"Just get up and come here, and you'll see."

He made a snort and got up, slowly and stiffly, and walked like an old man, holding himself very carefully. Keeping his upper body still. When he got to the door, I said, "Never mind."

He started to frown, but his eye hurt, so he stopped and swore at me. "Jesus Christ! What are you trying to do?"

"You been beat up," I said.

He forgot himself for a moment, turned sharply toward me, grunted with pain and put his hand against the wall to keep steady.

"Get out of here," he said as hard as he could without raising his voice.

"Somebody worked you over. I thought so when I saw the mouse, and I knew so when you tried to walk. You are in money trouble with someone Hawk works for and this is your second notice."

"You don't know what you're talking about."

"Yeah, I do. Hawk works that way. Lots of pressure on the body, where it doesn't show. Actually I'm surprised that there's any mark on your face."

"You're crazy," Shepard said. "I fell downstairs yesterday. Tripped on a rug. I don't owe anybody anything. I'm just doing business with Hawk."

I shook my head. "Hawk doesn't do business. It bores him. Hawk collects money, and guards bodies, that sort of thing. You're with him one day and the next you can hardly walk. Too big a coincidence. You better tell me."

Shepard had edged his way back to the desk and gotten seated. His hands shook a little as he folded them in front of him on the desk.

"You're fired," he said. "Get out of here. I'm going to sue you for every cent I gave you. You'll be hearing from my lawyer."

"Don't be a goddamned fool, Shepard. If you don't get out of what you're in, I'll be hearing from your embalmer. You got three kids and no wife. What happens to the kids if you get planted?"

Shepard made a weak attempt at a confident smile. "Listen, Spenser, I appreciate your concern, but this is a private matter, and it's nothing I can't handle. I'm a businessman, I know how to handle a business deal." His hands, clasped on the desk in front of him, were rigid, white-knuckled like his wife's had been on the New Bedford–Fairhaven bridge. Probably for the same reason. He was scared to death.

"One last try, Shepard. Are you doing business with King Powers?"

"I told you, Spenser, it is not your business." His voice did a chord change. "Stop trying to hustle yourself up some business. You and I are through. I want a check for five hundred dollars in the mail to me tomorrow or you'll find yourself in court." His voice was hitting the upper registers now. The tin clatter of hysteria.

"You know where to reach me," I said and walked out.

Living around Boston for a long time you tend to think of Cape Cod as the promised land. Sea, sun, sky, health, ease, boisterous camaraderie, a kind of real-life beer commercial. Since I'd arrived no one had liked me, and several people had told me to go away. Two had assaulted me. You're sure to fall in love with old Cape Cod.

I drove down to the end of Sea Street and parked illegally and walked on the beach. I seemed to be unemployed. There was no reason I could not pack up and go home. I looked at my watch. I could call Susan Silverman from the motel and in two hours we could be having a late lunch and going to the Museum of Fine Arts to look at the Vermeer exhibit that had just arrived. Giving Shepard back his retainer didn't thrill me, maybe Suze would pick up the lunch tab, but telling Shepard where his wife was didn't thrill me either.

I liked the idea of seeing Susan. I hadn't seen her in four days.

Lately I had found myself missing her when I didn't see her. It made me nervous.

The beach was crowded and a lot of kids were swimming off a float anchored fifty yards from shore. Down the curve of the beach there was a point and beyond I could see part of the Kennedy compound. I found some open beach and sat down and took off my shirt. A fat woman in a flowered bathing suit eyed the gun clipped to my belt. I took it off and wrapped it in the shirt and used the package for a pillow. The woman got up and folded her beach chair and moved to a different spot. At least people were consistent in their response. I closed my eyes and listened to the sound of the water and the children and occasionally a dog. Down the beach someone's portable radio was playing something about a man who'd been crying for a million years, so many tears. Where have you gone, Cole Porter?

It was a mess, too big a mess. I couldn't walk away from it. How big a mess, I didn't know, but a mess. More mess than even Shepard could handle, I thought.

I got up, clipped the gun back on my hip, stuck the holster in my hip pocket, put on my pale blue madras shirt with the epaulets and let it hang out to cover up the gun. I walked back to my car, got in and drove to my motel. It was nearly noontime.

From my room I called Susan Silverman at home. No answer. I went to the restaurant and had oyster stew and two draft beers and came back and called again. No answer. I called Deke Slade. He was in.

"Spenser," I said, "known in crime-detection circles as Mr. Sleuth."

"Yeah?"

"I have a couple of theories I'd like to share with you on some possible criminal activity in your jurisdiction. Want me to come in?"

"Criminal activity in my jurisdiction? You gotta stop watching those TV crime shows. You sound like Perry Mason."

"Just because you don't know how to talk right, Slade, is no reason to put me down. You want to hear my theories or not."

"Come on in," he said and hung up. He didn't sound excited.

11

"WHAT'S HAWK'S full name?" Slade said.

"I don't know," I said. "Just Hawk."

"He's gotta have a full name."

"Yeah, I know, but I don't know what it is. I've known him about twenty years and I've never heard him called anything but Hawk."

Slade shrugged and wrote Hawk on his pad of yellow, legal-sized lined paper. "Okay," he said. "So you figure that Shepard owes money and isn't paying and the guy he owes it to has sent a bone-breaker down. What's Shepard's story?"

"He has none," I said. "He says he's in business with Hawk and it's got nothing to do with me."

"And you don't believe him."

"Nope. First place Hawk doesn't do business, not that kind. He might sign on to kill somebody or steal something, or rescue somebody for that matter, but not business, with a big B like Shepard means. Hawk's a free spirit."

"Like you," Slade said.

I shook my head. "Nope, not like me. I don't hire out for the things Hawk does."

"I heard you might," Slade said.

"From who?"

"Oh, guys I know up in Boston. I made a couple of calls about you."

"I thought you were too busy keeping a close tail on the litterbugs," I said.

"I did it on my lunch hour," Slade said.

"Well, don't believe all you hear," I said.

Slade almost smiled. "Not likely," he said. "How sure are you he was beat up?"

"Shepard? Certain. I've seen it done before, fact I've had it done before. I know the look and feel of it."

"Yeah, it does stiffen you up some," Slade said. "What's Shepard's story?"

"Says he fell downstairs."

Slade wrote on his yellow pad again. "You got thoughts on who hired Hawk?"

"I'm guessing King Powers. Hawk normally gives first refusal to Powers." Slade wrote some more on his pad. "Powers is a shylock," I said. "Used to . . ."

"I know Powers," Slade said.

"Anyway, he's in trouble. Bad, I would guess, and he's too scared to yell for help."

"Or maybe too crooked."

I raised both eyebrows at Slade. "You know something I don't," I said.

Slade shook his head. "No, just wondering. Harv has always been very eager to get ahead. Not crooked really, just very ambitious. This leisure community he's building is causing a lot of hassle and it doesn't seem to be going up very fast, and people are beginning to wonder if something's wrong."

"Is there?"

"Hell," Slade said, "I don't know. You ever looked into a land swindle? It takes a hundred C.P.A.s and a hundred lawyers a hundred years just to find out if there's anything to look into." Slade made a disgusted motion with his mouth. "You usually can't find out who owns the goddamned property."

"Shepard doesn't strike me as crooked," I said.

"Adolf Hitler was fond of dogs," Slade said. "Say he's not crooked, say he's just overextended. Could be."

"Yeah," I said, "could be. But what are we going to do about it?"

"How the hell do I know. Am I the whiz-bang from the city?

You tell me. We got, to my knowledge, no crime, no victim, no violation of what you big-city types would call the criminal statutes. I'll have the patrol cars swing by his place more often and have everyone keep an eye out for him. I'll see if the A.G.'s office has anything on Shepard's land operation. You got any other thoughts?"

I shook my head.

"You find his wife?" Slade asked.

"Yeah."

"She coming home?"

"I don't think so."

"What's he going to do about that?"

"Nothing he can do."

"He can go get her and drag her ass home."

"He doesn't know where she is. I wouldn't tell him."

Slade frowned at me for about thirty seconds. "You are a pisser," Slade said. "I'll give you that."

"Yeah."

"Shepard take that okay?"

"No, he fired me. Told me he was going to sue me."

"So you're unemployed."

"I guess so."

"Just another tourist."

"Yep."

Slade did smile this time. A big smile that spread slowly across his face making deep furrows, one on each cheek. "Goddamn," he said and shook his head. "Goddamn."

I smiled back at him, warmly, got up and left. Back in my car, on the hot seats, with the top down, I thought something I've thought before. I don't know what to do, I thought. I started the car, turned on the radio and sat with the motor idling. I didn't even know where to go. Mrs. Shepard sure wasn't happy, and Mr. Shepard sure wasn't happy. That didn't make them unusual of course. I wasn't right at the moment all that goddamned happy myself. I supposed I ought to go home. Home's where you can go and they have to take you in. Who said that? I couldn't remember. Cynical bastard though. I put the car in gear and drove slowly down Main Street toward the motel. Course at my home there wasn't any they. There was just me. I'd take me in any time. I stopped for a light. A red-haired girl wearing powder blue flared denim slacks and a lime-colored halter top strolled by. The slacks were so tight I could see the brief line of her underpants slanting across her buttocks. She looked at the car in a friendly fashion. I could offer her a drink and a swim and dazzle her with my Australian crawl. But she looked like a college kid and she'd probably want me to do some dope and rap about the need for love and a new consciousness. The light turned green and I moved on. A middle-aged grump with nowhere to go. It was a little after one when I pulled into the parking lot at my motel. Time for lunch. With renewed vigor I strode into the lobby, turned left past the desk and headed down the corridor toward my room. A fast wash, and then on to lunch. Who'd have thought but moments ago that I was without purpose. When I opened the door to my room Susan Silverman was lying on the bed reading a book by Erik Erikson and looking like she should.

I said, "Jesus Christ, I'm glad to see you."

With her finger in the book to keep her place she turned her head toward me and said, "Likewise, I'm sure" and grinned. Often she smiled, but sometimes she didn't smile, she grinned. This was a grin. I never knew for sure what the difference was but it had something to do with gleeful wickedness. Her smile was beautiful and good, but in her grin there was just a hint of evil. I dove on top of her on the bed, breaking the impact of my weight with my arms, and grabbed her and hugged her.

"Ow," she said. I eased up a little on the hug, and we kissed each other. When we stopped I said, "I am not going to ask how you got in here because I know that you can do anything you want to, and getting the management to aid and abet you in a B and E would be child's play for you."

"Child's play," she said. "How has it been with you, blue eyes?"

We lay on our backs on the bed beside each other while I told her. When I finished telling her I suggested an afternoon of sensual delight, starting now. But she suggested that it start after lunch and after a brief scuffle I agreed.

"Suze," I said in the dining room starting my first stein of

Harp while she sipped a Margarita, "you seemed uncommonly amused by the part where Jane tried to caponize me."

She laughed. "I think your hips are beginning to widen out," she said. "Are you still shaving?"

"Naw," I said, "it did no damage. If it had, all the waitresses here would be wearing black armbands and the flag would fly half-mast at Radcliffe."

"Well, we'll see, later, when there's nothing better to do."

"There's never anything better to do," I said. She yawned elaborately.

The waitress came and took our order. When she'd departed Susan said, "What are you going to do?"

"Jesus, I don't know."

"Want me to hang around with you while you do it?"

"Very much," I said. "I think I'm in over my head with Pam, Rose and Jane."

"Good, I brought my suitcase on the chance you might want me to stay."

"Yeah, and I noted you unpacked it and hung up your clothes. Confidence."

"Oh, you noticed. I keep forgetting you are a detective."

"Spenser's the name, clues are my game," I said. The waitress brought me a half-dozen oysters and Susan six soused shrimp. Susan looked at the oysters.

"Trying to make a comeback?"

"No," I said, "planning ahead."

We ate our seafood.

"What makes you say you're in over your head?" Susan asked.

"I don't feel easy. It's an element I'm not comfortable in. I'm good with my hands, and I'm persevering, but . . . Pam Shepard asked me if I had children and I said no. And she said I probably couldn't understand, and she asked if I were married and I said no and she said then for sure I couldn't understand." I shrugged.

"I've never had children either," Susan said. "And marriage wasn't the best thing that ever happened to me. Nor the most permanent. I don't know. There's all the cliché's about you don't have to be able to cook a soufflé to know when one's bad. But . . .

at school, I know, parents come in sometimes for counseling with the kids and they say, but you don't know. You don't have children . . . there's probably something to it. Say there is. So what? You've been involved in a lot of things that you haven't experienced firsthand, as I recall. Why is this one different?"

"I don't know that it is," I said.

"I think it is. I've never heard you talk about things like this before. On a scale of ten you normally test out about fifteen in confidence."

"Yeah, I think it is too."

"Of course, as you explain it, the case is no longer your business because the case no longer exists."

"There's that," I said.

"Then why worry about it. If it's not your element, anyway, why not settle for that. We'll eat and swim and walk on the beach for a few days and go home."

The waitress came with steak for each of us, and salad, and rolls and another beer for me. We ate in silence for maybe two minutes.

"I can't think of anything else to do," I said.

"Try to control your enthusiasm," Susan said.

"I'm sorry," I said. "I didn't mean it that way. It's just bothering me. I've been with two people whose lives are screwed up to hell and I can't seem to get them out of it at all."

"Of course you can't," she said. "You also can't do a great deal about famine, war, pestilence and death."

"A great backfield," I said.

"You also can't be everyone's father. It is paternalistic of you to assume that Pam Shepard with the support of several other women cannot work out her own future without you. She may in fact do very well. I have."

"Me paternalistic? Don't be absurd. Eat your steak and shut up or I'll spank you."

12

AFTER LUNCH we took coffee on the terrace by the pool, sitting at a little white table made of curlicued iron covered by a blue and white umbrella. It was mostly kids in the pool, splashing and yelling while their mothers rubbed oil on their legs. Susan Silverman was sipping coffee from a cup she held with both hands and looking past me. I saw her eyes widen behind her lavender sunglasses and I turned and there was Hawk.

He said, "Spenser."

I said, "Hawk."

He said, "Mind if I join you?"

I said, "Have a seat. Susan, this is Hawk. Hawk, this is Susan Silverman."

Hawk smiled at her and she said, "Hello, Hawk."

Hawk pulled a chair around from the next table, and sat with us. Behind him was a big guy with a sunburned face and an Oriental dragon tattooed on the inside of his left forearm. As Hawk pulled his chair over he nodded at the next table and the tattooed man sat down at it. "That's Powell," Hawk said. Powell didn't say anything. He just sat with his arms folded and stared at us.

"Coffee?" I said to Hawk.

He nodded. "Make it iced coffee though." I gestured to the waitress, ordered Hawk his iced coffee.

"Hawk," I said, "you gotta overcome this impulse toward anonymity you've got. I mean why not start to dress so people will notice you instead of always fading into the background like you do."

"I'm just a retiring guy, Spenser, just my nature." He stressed the first syllable in retiring. "Don't see no reason to be a clotheshorse." Hawk was wearing white Puma track shoes with a black slash on them. White linen slacks, and a matching white linen vest with no shirt. Powell was more conservatively dressed in a maroon-and-yellow-striped tank top and maroon slacks.

The waitress brought Hawk his iced coffee. "You and Susan having a vacation down here?"

"Yep."

"Sure is nice, isn't it? Always like the Cape. Got atmosphere you don't usually find. You know? Hard to define it, but it's a kind of leisure spirit. Don't you think, Spenser?"

"Yeah, leisure spirit. That what brought you down here, Hawk?"

"Oh, something like that. Had a chance to get in what you might call a working vacation. How 'bout yourself? Doing a little work for Harv Shepard?"

"I'll tell you if you'll tell me."

"Susan," Hawk said, "this man is a straight-ahead man, you know? Just puts it right out front, hell of a quality, I'd say."

Susan smiled at him and nodded. He smiled back.

"Come on, Hawk, knock off the Goody Two-shoes shtick. You want to know what I'm doing with Shepard and I want to know what you're doing with Shepard."

"Actually, it's a little more than that, babe, or a little less, whichever way you look at it. It ain't that I so much care what you're doing with Shepard as it is I want you to stop doing it."

"Ah-ha," I said. "A threat. That explains why you brought Eric the Red along. You knew Susan was with me and you didn't want to be outnumbered."

Powell said from his table, "What did you call me?"

Hawk smiled. "Still got that agile mind, Spenser."

Powell said again, "What did you call me?"

"It is hard, Powell," I said to him, "to look tough when your nose is peeling. Why not try some Sun Ban, excellent, greaseless, filters out the harmful ultraviolet rays."

Powell stood up. "Don't smart-mouth me, man. You wising off at me?"

"That a picture of your mom you got tattooed on your left arm?" I said.

He looked down at the dragon tattoo on his forearm for a minute and then back at me. His face got redder and he said, "You wise bastard. I'm going to straighten you out right now."

Hawk said, "Powell, I wouldn't if I was you."

"I don't have to take a lot of shit from a guy like this," Powell said.

"Don't swear in front of the lady," Hawk said. "You gotta take about whatever he gives you 'cause you can't handle him."

"He don't look so tough to me," Powell said. He was standing and people around the pool were beginning to look.

"That's 'cause you are stupid, Powell," Hawk said. "He is tough, he may be damn near as tough as me. But you want to try him, go ahead."

Powell reached down and grabbed me by the shirt front. Susan Silverman inhaled sharply.

Hawk said, "Don't kill him, Spenser, he runs errands for me."

Powell yanked me out of the chair. I went with the yank and hit him in the Adam's apple with my forearm. He said something like "ark" and let go of my shirt front and stepped back. I hit him with two left hooks, the second one with a lot of shoulder turned into it, and Powell fell over backward into the pool. Hawk was grinning as I turned toward him.

"The hayshakers are all the same, aren't they," he said. "Just don't seem to know the difference between amateurs and professionals." He shook his head. "That's a good lady you got there though." He nodded at Susan, who was on her feet holding a beer bottle she'd apparently picked up off another table.

Hawk got up and walked to the pool and dragged Powell out of it negligently, with one hand, as if the dead weight of a 200-pound man were no more than a flounder.

The silence around the pool was heavy. The kids were still hanging on to the edge of the pool, staring at us. Hawk said, "Come on, let's walk out to my car and talk." He let Powell slump to the ground by the table and strolled back in through the lobby. Susan and I went with him. As we passed the desk we saw the manager come out of his office and hurry toward the terrace.

I said, "Why don't you go down the room, Suze. I'll be along in a minute. Hawk just wants me to give him some pointers on poolside fighting." The tip of her tongue was stuck out through her closed mouth and she was obviously biting on it. "Don't bite your tongue," I said. "Save some for me." She shook her head.

"I'll stay with you," she said.

Hawk opened the door on the passenger's side of the Cadillac. "My pleasure," he said to Susan. If Hawk and I were going to fight he wouldn't pick a convertible for the place. I got in after Susan. Hawk went around and got in the driver's side. He pushed a button and the roof went up smoothly. He started the engine and turned on the air conditioning. A blue and white Barnstable Township police car pulled into the parking lot and two cops got out and walked into the motel.

Hawk said, "Let's ride around." I nodded and he put us in gear and slipped out of the parking lot.

"Where the hell did you get him?" I said to Hawk as we drove.

"Powell? Oh, man, I don't know. He's a local dude. People that hired me told me to work with him."

"They trying to set up an apprentice program?"

Hawk shrugged. "Beats me, baby, he got a long way to go though, don't he."

"It bother you that the cops are going to ask him what he was doing fighting with a tourist, and who the tourist was and who was the black stud in the funny outfit?"

Hawk shook his head. "He won't say nothing. He dumb, but he ain't that dumb."

Between us on the front seat Susan Silverman said, "What are we doing?"

Hawk laughed. "A fair question, Susan. What in hell are we doing?"

"Let me see if I can guess," I said. "I guess that Harv Shepard owes money to a man, probably King Powers, and Hawk has been asked to collect it. Or maybe just oversee the disbursement of funds, whatever, and that things are going the way they should." I said to Susan, "Hawk does this stuff, quite well. And then surprise, I appear, and I'm working for Shepard. And Hawk and his employer, probably King Powers, wonder if Harv hired me to counteract Hawk. So Hawk has dropped by to inquire about my relationship with Harv Shepard, and to urge me to sever that relationship."

The Caddie went almost soundless along the Mid-Cape Highway, down Cape, toward Provincetown. I said, "How close, Hawk?"

He shrugged. "I have explained to the people that employ me about how you are. I don't expect to frighten you away, and I don't expect to bribe you, but my employer would like to compensate you for any loss if you were to withdraw from the case."

"Hawk," I said. "All this time I've known you I never could figure out why sometimes you talk like an account exec from Merrill Lynch and sometimes you talk like Br'er Bear."

"Ah is the product of a ghetto education." He pronounced both t's in ghetto. "Sometimes my heritage keep popping up."

"Lawdy me, yes," I said. "What part of the ghetto you living in now?"

Hawk grinned at Susan. "Beacon Hill," he said. He U-turned the Caddie over the center strip and headed back up Cape toward Hyannis. "Anyway, I told the people you weren't gonna do what they wanted, whatever I said, but they give me money to talk to you, so I'm talking. What your interest in Shepard?"

"He hired me to look for his wife."

"That all?"

"That's all."

"You find her?"

"Yes."

"Where?"

"I won't say."

"Don't matter, Shepard'll tell me. If I need to know."

"No." I shook my head. "He doesn't know either."

"You won't tell him?"

"Nope."

"Why not, man. That's what you hired on for."

"She doesn't want to be found."

Hawk shook his head again. "You complicate your life, Spenser. You think about things too much."

"That's one of the things that makes me not you, Hawk."

"Maybe," Hawk said, "and maybe you a lot more like me than you want to say. 'Cept you ain't as good looking."

"Yeah, but I dress better."

Hawk snorted, "Shit. Excuse me, Susan. Anyway, my problem now is whether I believe you. It sounds right. Sounds just about your speed, Spenser. Course you ain't just fell off the sugar-beet truck going through town, and if you was lying it would sound good. You still work for Shepard?"

"No, he canned me. He says he's going to sue me."

"Ah wouldn't worry all that much about the suing," Hawk said. "Harv's kinda busy."

"Is it Powers?" I said.

"Maybe it is, maybe it ain't. You gonna stay out of this, Spenser?"

"Maybe I will, maybe I won't."

Hawk nodded. We drove a way in silence.

"Who's King Powers?" Susan said.

"A thief," I said. "Loan sharking, numbers, prostitution, laundromats, motels, trucking, produce, Boston, Brockton, Fall River, New Bedford."

Hawk said, "Not Brockton anymore. Angie Degamo has got Brockton now."

"Angie chase Powers out?"

"Naw, some kind of business deal. I wasn't in it."

"Anyway," I said to Susan, "Powers is like that."

"And you work for him," she said to Hawk.

"Some."

"Hawk's a free-lance," I said. "But Powers asks him early when he's got Hawk's kind of work."

"And what is Hawk's kind of work?" Susan said, still to Hawk.

"He does muscle and gun work."

"Ah prefer the term soldier of fortune, honey," Hawk said to me.

"Doesn't it bother you," Susan said, "to hurt people for money?"

"No more than it does him." Hawk nodded to me.

"I don't think he does it for money," she said.

"Tha's why Ah'm bopping down the Cape in a new El Dorado and he's driving that eight-year-old hog with the gray tape on the upholstery."

"But ..." Susan looked for the right words. "But he does what he must, his aim is to help. Yours is to hurt."

"Not right," Hawk said. "Maybe he aiming to help. But he also like the work. You know? I mean he could be a social worker if he just want to help. I get nothing out of hurting people. Sometimes just happens that way. Just don't be so sure me and old Spenser are so damn different, Susan."

We pulled back into the parking lot at the motel. The blue and white was gone. I said, "You people through discussing me yet, I got a couple things to say, but I don't want to interrupt. The subject is so goddamned fascinating."

Susan just shook her head.

"Okay," I said. "This is straight, Hawk. I'm not working for Shepard, or anybody, at the moment. But I can't go home and let you and Powers do what you want. I'm gonna hang around, I think, and see if I can get you off Shepard's back."

Hawk looked at me without expression. "That's what I told them," he said. "I told them that's what you'd say if I came around and talked. But they paying the money. I'll tell them I was right. I don't think it gonna scare them."

"I didn't suppose it would," I said.

I opened the door and got out and held it open for Susan. She slid out, and then leaned back in and spoke to Hawk. "Goodby," she said. "I'm not sure what to say. Glad to have met you wouldn't do, exactly. But" — she shrugged — "thanks for the ride."

Hawk smiled at her. "My pleasure, Susan. Maybe I'll see you again."

I closed the door and Hawk slid the car out of the parking lot, soundless and smooth, like a shark cruising in still water.

13

SUSAN SAID, "I want a drink."

We went in and sat on two barstools, at the corner, where the bar turns. Susan ordered a martini and I had a beer. "Martini?" I said.

She nodded. "I said I wanted a drink. I meant it." She drank half the martini in a single pull and put the glass back on the bar. "How different?" she said, and looked at me.

"You mean me and Hawk?"

"Uh huh."

"I don't know. I don't beat people up for money. I don't kill people for money. He does."

"But sometimes you'll do it for nothing. Like this afternoon."

"Powell?"

"Powell. You didn't have to fight him. You needled him into it."

I shrugged.

"Didn't you?" Susan said.

I shrugged again. She belted back the rest of the martini. "Why?"

I gestured the bartender down. "Another round," I said.

We were silent while he put the martini together and drew the beer and placed them before us.

"Got any peanuts," I said.

He nodded and brought a bowl up from under the bar. The

place was almost deserted, a couple having a late lunch across the room, and four guys, who looked like they'd been golfing, drinking mixed drinks at a table behind us. Susan sipped at her second martini.

"How can you drink those things?" I said. "They taste like a toothache cure."

"It's how I prove I'm tough," she said.

"Oh," I said. I ate some of the peanuts. The voices of the golf foursome were loud. Full of jovial good fellowship like the voice of a game-show host. A little desperate.

"Millions of guys spend their lives that way," I said. "Sitting around pretending to be a good fellow with guys they have nothing to say to."

Susan nodded. "Not just guys," she said.

"I always thought women did that better though," I said.

"Early training," Susan said, "at being a phony, so men would like you. You going to answer my question?"

"About why I badgered Powell?"

"Uh huh."

"You don't give up easy, do you?"

"Un unh."

"I don't know exactly why I pushed him. He annoyed me sitting there, but it also seemed about the right move to make at the time."

"To show Hawk you weren't afraid?"

"No, I don't think it impressed Hawk one way or the other. It was a gut reaction. A lot of what I do is a gut reaction. You're a linear thinker, you want to know why and how come and what the source of the problem is and how to work out a solution to it. I assume it comes, in part, with being a guidance type."

"You're reversing the stereotype, you know," Susan said.

"What? Women emotional, men rational? Yeah. But that was always horseshit anyway. Mostly, I think it's just the opposite. In my case anyway. I don't think in ABC order. I've gotten to be over forty and done a lot of things, and I've learned to trust my impulses usually. I tend to perceive in images and patterns and — what to call it — whole situations."

"Gestalt," Susan said.

"Whatever, so when you say why I feel like the best I can do is describe the situation. If I had a video tape of the situation I would point at it and say, 'See, that's why.'"

"Would you have done the same thing if I weren't there?"

"You mean was I showing off?" The bartender came down and looked at our glasses. I nodded and he took them away for refill. "Maybe." The bartender brought the drinks back. "Would you have hit someone with that beer bottle if I needed it?"

"You insufferable egotist," Susan said. "Why don't you think I picked the bottle up to defend myself?"

"You got me," I said. "I never thought of that. Is that why you picked it up?"

"No," she said. "And stop grinning like a goddamned idiot." She drank some of her third martini. "Smug bastard," she said.

"You did it because I'm such terrific tail, didn't you."

"No," she said. The force of her face and eyes were on me. "I did it because I love you."

The couple across the room got up from the table and headed out. She was Clairol blond, her hair stiff and brittle, he was wearing white loafers and a matching belt. As they left the dining room their hands brushed and he took hers and held it. I drank the rest of my beer. Susan sipped at her martini. "Traditionally," she said, "the gentleman's response to that remark is, 'I love you too.'" She wasn't looking at me now. She was studying the olive in the bottom of her martini.

"Suze," I said. "Do we have to complicate it?"

"You can't say the traditional thing?"

"It's not saying 'I love you,' it's what comes after."

"You mean love and marriage, they go together like a horse and carriage?"

I shrugged. "I don't suppose they have to, I've seen a lot of marriages without love. I guess it could work the other way."

Susan said, "Um hum" and looked at me steadily again.

"The way we're going now seems nice," I said.

"No," she said. "It is momentary and therefore finally pointless. It has no larger commitment, it involves no risk, and therefore no real relationship."

"To have a real relationship you gotta suffer?"

"You have to risk it," she said. "You have to know that if it gets homely and unpleasant you can't just walk away."

"And that means marriage? Lots of people walk away from marriage. For crissake, I got a lady client at this moment who has done just that."

"After what, twenty-two years?" Susan said.

"One point for your side," I said. "She didn't run off at the first sprinkle of rain, did she. But does that make the difference? Some J.P. reading from the Bible?"

"No," Susan said. "But the ceremony is the visible symbol of the commitment. We ritualize our deepest meanings usually, and marriage is the way we've ritualized love. Or one of the ways."

"Are you saying we should get married?"

"At the moment I'm saying I love you and I'm waiting for a response."

"It's not that simple, Suze."

"And I believe I've gotten the response." She got up from the bar and walked out. I finished my beer, left a ten on the bar and walked back to my room. She wasn't there. She also was not on the terrace or in the lobby or in the parking lot. I looked for her small blue Chevy Nova and didn't see it. I went back to the room. Her suitcase was still on the rack, her clothes hanging in the closet. She wouldn't go home without her clothes. Without me maybe, but not without her clothes. I sat down on the bed and looked at the red chair in the corner. The seat was one form of molded plastic, the legs four thin rounds of dark wood with little brass booties on the bottom. Elegant. I was much too damn big and tough to cry. Too old also. It wasn't that goddamned simple.

On the top of the bureau was a card that said, "Enjoy our health club and sauna." I got undressed, dug a pair of white shorts and a gray T-shirt out of the bureau, put them on and laced up my white Adidas track shoes with the three black stripes, no socks. Susan always bitched at me about no socks when we played tennis, but I liked the look. Besides, it was a bother putting socks on.

The health club was one level down, plaid-carpeted, several rooms, facilities for steam, sauna, rubdowns, and an exercise room with a Universal Trainer. A wiry middle-aged man in white slacks and a white T-shirt gave me a big smile when I came in.

"Looking for a nice workout, sir?"

"Yeah."

"Well, we've got the equipment. You familiar with a Universal, sir?"

"Yeah."

"It is, as you can see, a weightlifting machine that operates on pulleys and runs, thus allowing a full workout without the time-consuming inconvenience of changing plates on a barbell."

"I know," I said.

"Let me give you an idea of how ours works. There are eight positions on the central unit here, the bench press, curls, over-the-head press . . ."

"I know," I said.

"The weight numbering on the left is beginning weight, the markings on the right are overload weights resulting from the diminishment of fulcrum . . ."

I got on the bench, shoved the pin into the slot marked 300, took a big breath and blew the weight up to arm's length and let it back. I did it two more times.

The trainer said, "I guess you've done this before."

"Yeah," I said.

He went back toward the trainer's room. "You want anything, you let me know," he said.

I moved to the lat machine, did 15 pull downs with 150, did 15 tricep presses with 90, moved to the curl bar, then to the bench again. I didn't normally lift that heavy on the bench but I needed to bust a gut or something and 300-pound bench presses were just right for that. I did four sets of everything and the sweat was soaking through my shirt and running down the insides of my arms, so I had to keep wiping my hands to keep a grip on the weight bars. I finished up doing twenty-five dips, and when I stepped away my arms were trembling and my breath was coming in gasps. It was a slow day for the health club. I was the only one in there, and the trainer had come out after a while and watched.

"Hey," he said, "you really work out, don't you?"

"Yeah," I said. There was a heavy bag in one corner of the training room. "You got gloves for that thing?" I said.

"Got some speed gloves," the trainer said.

"Gimme," I said.

He brought them out and I put them on and leaned against the wall, getting my breath under control and waiting for my arms to stop feeling rubbery. It didn't used to take as long. In about five minutes, I was ready for the bag. I stood close to it, maybe six inches away, and punched it in combinations as hard as I could. Two lefts, a right. Left jab, left hook, right cross, left jab, left jab, step-back right uppercut. It's hard to hit a heavy bag with an uppercut. It has no chin. I hit the bag for as long as I could, as hard as I could. Grunting with the effort. Staying up against it and trying to get all the power I could into the six-inch punches. If you've never done it you have no idea how tiring it is to punch something. Every couple of minutes I had to back away and lean on the wall and recover.

The trainer said to me, "You used to fight?"

"Yeah," I said.

"You can always tell," he said. "Everybody comes in here slaps at the bag, or gives it a punch. They can't resist it. But one guy in a hundred actually hits it and knows what he's doing."

"Yeah." I went back to the bag, driving my left fist into it, alternating jabs and hooks, trying to punch through it. The sweat rolled down my face and dripped from my arms and legs. My shirt was soaking and I was beginning to see black spots dancing like visions of sugar plums before my eyes.

"You want some salt?" the trainer said. I shook my head. My gray T-shirt was soaked black with sweat. Sweat ran down my arms and legs. My hair was dripping wet. I stepped back from the bag and leaned on the wall. My breath was heaving in and out and my arms were numb and rubbery. I slid my back down the wall and sat on the floor, knees up, back against the wall, my forearms resting on my knees, my head hanging, and waited while the breath got under control and the spots went away. The speed gloves were slippery with sweat as I peeled them off. I got up and handed them to the trainer.

"Thanks," I said.

"Sure," he said. "When you work out, man, you work out, don't you?"

"Yeah," I said.

I walked slowly out of the training room and up the stairs. Several people looked at me as I crossed the lobby toward my room. The floor of the lobby was done in rust-colored quarry tile, about 8" x 8". In my room I turned up the air conditioner and took a shower, standing a long time under the hard needle spray. Susan's make-up kit was still on the vanity. I toweled dry, put on a blue and white tank top, white slacks and black loafers. I looked at my gun lying on the bureau. "Screw it." I headed clean and tired and unarmed down the corridor, back to the bar, and began to drink bourbon.

14

I WOKE UP at eight-fifteen the next morning feeling like a failed suicide. The other bed had not been slept in. At twenty to nine I got out of bed and shuffled to the bathroom, took two aspirin and another shower. At nine-fifteen I walked stiffly and slow down to the coffee shop and drank two large orange juices and three cups of black coffee. At ten of ten I walked less stiffly, but still slow, back to my room and called my answering service. In desperate times, habit helps give form to our lives.

Pam Shepard had called and would call again. "She said it was urgent, Spenser."

"Thank you, Lillian. When she calls again give her this number." I hung up and waited. Ten minutes later the phone rang.

"Spenser," I said.

"I need help," she said. "I've got to talk with you."

"Talk," I said.

"I don't want to talk on the phone, I need to see you, and be with you when I talk. I'm scared. I don't know who else to call."

"Okay, I'll come up to your place."

"No, we're not there anymore. Do you know where Plimoth Plantation is?"

"Yes."

"I'll meet you there. Walk down the main street of the village. I'll see you."

"Okay, I'll leave now. See you there about noon?"

"Yes. I mustn't be found. Don't let anyone know you're going to see me. Don't let anyone follow you."

"You want to give me a hint of what your problem is?"

"No," she said. "Just meet me where we said."

"I'll be there."

We hung up. It was ten-thirty. Shouldn't take more than half an hour to drive to Plymouth. Susan's clothes were still in the closet. She'd come back for them, and the make-up kit. She must have been incensed beyond reason to have left that. She'd probably checked into another motel. Maybe even another room in this one. I could wait an hour. Maybe she'd come back for her clothes. I got a piece of stationery and an envelope from the drawer of the desk, wrote a note, sealed it in the envelope and wrote Susan's name on the outside. I got Susan's cosmetic case from the bathroom and put it on the desk. I propped the note against it, and sat down in a chair near the bathroom door.

At eleven-thirty someone knocked softly on my door. I got up and stepped into the bathroom, out of sight, behind the open bathroom door. Another knock. A wait. And then a key in the lock. Through the crack of the hinge end of the bathroom door I could see the motel room door open. Susan came in. Must have gotten the key at the desk. Probably said she'd lost hers. She walked out of sight toward the desk top where the note was. I heard her tear open the envelope. The note said, "Lurking in the bathroom is a horse's ass. It requires the kiss of a beautiful woman to turn him into a handsome prince again." I stepped out from behind the door, into the room. Susan put the note down, turned and saw me. With no change of expression she walked over and gave me a small kiss on the mouth. Then she stepped back and studied me closely. She shook her head. "Didn't work," she said. "You're still a horse's ass."

"It was the low-voltage kiss," I said. "Transforming a horse's ass into a handsome prince is a high-intensity task."

"I'll try once more," she said. And put both arms around me and kissed me hard on the mouth. The kiss held, and developed into much more and relaxed in postclimactic languor without a sound. Without even breaking the kiss. At close range I could see Susan's eyes still closed.

I took my mouth from hers and said, "You wanta go to Plimoth Plantation?"

Susan opened her eyes and looked at me. "Anywhere at all," she said. "You are still a horse's ass, but you are my horse's ass."

I said, "I love you."

She closed her eyes again and pushed her face against the hollow of my neck and shoulder for a moment. Then she pulled her head back and opened her eyes and nodded her head. "Okay, prince," she said. "Let's get to Plimoth."

Our clothes were in a scattered tangle on the floor and by the time we sorted them out and got them back on it was noon. "We are late," I said.

"I hurried as fast as I could," Susan said. She was putting on her lipstick in the mirror, bending way over the dresser to do it.

"We were fast," I said. "A half-hour from horse's ass to handsome prince. I think that fulfills the legal definition of a quickie."

"You're the one in a hurry to go see Plimoth Plantation. Given the choice between sensual delight and historical restoration, I'd have predicted a different decision on your part."

"I've got to see someone there, and it may help if you're with me. Perhaps later we can reconsider the choice."

"I'm ready," she said. And we went out of the room to my car. On the drive up Route 3 to Plymouth I told Susan what little I knew about why we were going.

Susan said, "Won't she panic or something if I show up with you? She did say something about alone."

"We won't go in together," I said. "When I find her, I'll explain who you are and introduce you. You been to the Plantation before?"

She nodded. "Well, then, you can just walk down the central street a bit ahead of me and hang around till I holler."

"Always the woman's lot," she said.

I grunted. A sign on my left said Plimoth Plantation Road and I turned in. The road wound up through a meadow toward a stand of pines. Behind the pines was a parking lot and at one edge of the parking lot was a ticket booth. I parked and Susan got out and walked ahead, bought a ticket and went through the entrance. When she was out of sight I got out and did the same thing. Beyond the ticket booth was a rustic building containing a gift shop, lunch room and information service. I went on past it and headed down the soft path between the high pines toward the Plantation itself. A few years back I had been reading Samuel Eliot Morison's big book of American history, and got hooked and drove around the east going to Colonial restorations. Williamsburg is the most dazzling, and Sturbridge is grand, but Plimoth Plantation is always a small pleasure.

I rounded the curve by the administration building and saw the blockhouse of dark wood and the stockade around the little town and beyond it the sea. The area was entirely surrounded by woods and if you were careful you could see no sign of the twentieth century. If you weren't careful and looked too closely you could see Bert's Restaurant and somebody else's motel down along the shore. But for a moment I could go back, as I could every time I came, to the small cluster of zealous Christians in the wilderness of seventeenth-century America, and experience a sense of the desolation they must have felt, minute and remote and resolute in the vast woods.

I saw Susan on top of the blockhouse, looking out at the village, her arms folded on the parapet, and I came back to business and walked up the hill, past the blockhouse and into the Plantation. There was one street, narrow and rutted, leading downhill toward the ocean. Thatched houses along each side, behind the herb gardens, some livestock and a number of people dressed in Colonial costume. Lots of children, lots of Kodak Instamatics. I walked down the hill, slowly, letting Pam Shepard have ample time to spot me and see that I wasn't followed. I went the whole length of the street and started back up. As I passed Myles Standish's house, Pam came out of the door wearing huge sunglasses and fell into step beside me.

"You're alone."

"No, I have a friend with me. A woman." It seemed important to say it was a woman.

"Why," she said. Her eyes were wide and dark.

"You are in trouble, and maybe she could help. She's an A-1 woman. And I had the impression you weren't into men much lately."

"Can I trust her?"

"Yes."

"Can I trust you?"

"Yes."

"I suppose you wouldn't say so if I couldn't anyway, would you?" She was wearing a faded denim pants and jacket combo over a funky-looking multicolored T-shirt. She was exactly as immaculate and neat and fresh-from-the-shower-and-make-up-table as she had been the last time I saw her.

"No, I wouldn't. Come on, I'll introduce you to my friend, then we can go someplace and sit down and maybe have a drink or a snack or both and talk about whatever you'd like to talk about."

She looked all around her as if she might dart back into one of the thatched houses and hide in the loft. Then she took a deep breath and said, "Okay, but I mustn't be seen."

"Seen by who?"

"By anyone, by anyone who would recognize me."

"Okay, we'll get Susan and we'll go someplace obscure." I walked back up the street toward the gate to the blockhouse, Pam Shepard close by me as if trying to stay in my shadow. Near the top of the hill Susan Silverman met us. I nodded at her and she smiled.

"Pam Shepard," I said. "Susan Silverman." Susan put out her hand and smiled.

Pam Shepard said, "Hello."

I said, "Come on, we'll head back to the car."

In the car Pam Shepard talked with Susan. "Are you a detective too, Susan?"

"No, I'm a guidance counselor at Smithfield High School," Susan said.

"Oh, really? That must be very interesting."

"Yes," Susan said, "it is. It's tiresome, sometimes, like most things, but I love it."

"I never worked," Pam said. "I always just stayed home with the kids."

"But that must be interesting too," Susan said. "And tiresome. I never had much chance to do that."

"You're not married?"

"Not now, I was divorced quite some time ago."

"Children?"

Susan shook her head. I pulled into the parking lot at Bert's. "You know anybody in this town," I said to Pam.

"No."

"Okay, then this place ought to be fairly safe. It doesn't look like a spot people would drive up from the Cape to go to."

Bert's was a two-story building done in weathered shingles fronting on the ocean. Inside, the dining room was bright, pleasant, informal and not very full. We sat by the window and looked at the waves come in and go out. The waitress came. Susan didn't want a drink. Pam Shepard had a stinger on the rocks. I ordered a draft beer. The waitress said they had none. "I've learned," I said, "to live with disappointment." The waitress said she could bring me a bottle of Heinekens. I said it would do. The menu leaned heavily toward fried seafood. Not my favorite, but the worst meal I ever had was wonderful. At least they didn't feature things like the John Alden Burger or Pilgrim Soup.

The waitress brought the drinks and took our food order. I drank some of my Heinekens. "Okay, Mrs. Shepard," I said. "What's up?"

She looked around. There was no one near us. She drank some of her stinger. "I . . . I'm involved in a murder."

I nodded. Susan sat quietly with her hands folded in front of her on the table.

"We . . . there was . . ." She took another gulp of the stinger. "We robbed a bank in New Bedford, and the bank guard, an old man with a red face, he . . . Jane shot him and he's dead."

The tide was apparently ebbing. The high mark was traced close to the restaurant by an uneven line of seaweed and driftwood and occasional scraps of rubbish. Much cleaner than New Bedford harbor. I wondered what flotsam was. I'd have to look that up sometime when I got home. And jetsam.

"What bank?" I said.

"Bristol Security," she said. "On Kempton Street."

"Were you identified?"

"I don't know. I was wearing these sunglasses."

"Okay, that's a start. Take them off."

"But . . ."

"Take them off, they're no longer a disguise, they are an identification." She reached up quickly and took them off and put them in her purse.

"Not in your purse, give them to me." She did, and I slipped them in Susan Silverman's purse. "We'll ditch them on the way out," I said.

"I never thought," she said.

"No, probably you don't have all that much experience at robbery and murder. You'll get better as you go along."

Susan said, "Spenser."

I said, "Yeah, I know. I'm sorry."

"I didn't know," Pam Shepard said. "I didn't know Jane would really shoot. I just went along. It seemed . . . it seemed I ought to — they'd stood by me and all."

Susan was nodding. "And you felt you had to stand by them. Anyone would."

The waitress brought the food, crab salad for Susan, lobster stew for Pam, fisherman's plate for me. I ordered another beer.

"What was the purpose of the robbery?" Susan said.

"We needed money for guns."

"Jesus Christ," I said.

"Rose and Jane are organizing . . . I shouldn't tell you this . . ."

"Babe," I said, "you better goddamned well tell me everything you can think of. If you want me to get your ass out of this."

Susan frowned at me.

"Don't be mad at me," Pam Shepard said.

"Bullshit," I said. "You want me to bring you flowers for being a goddamn thief and a murderer? Sweets for the sweet, my love. Hope the old guy didn't have an old wife who can't get along without him. Once you all get guns you can liberate her too."

Susan said, "Spenser," quite sharply. "She feels bad enough."

"No she doesn't," I said. "She doesn't feel anywhere near bad enough. Neither do you. You're so goddamned empathetic you've jumped into her frame. 'And you felt you had to stand by them. Anyone would.' Balls. Anyone wouldn't. You wouldn't."

I snarled at Pam Shepard. "How about it. You thought you were going to a dance recital when you went into that bank with guns to steal the money? You thought you were Faye Dunaway, la de da, we'll take the money and run and the theme music will come up and the banjos will play and all the shots will miss?" I bit a fried shrimp in half. Not bad. Tears were rolling down Pam Shepard's face. Susan looked very grim. But she was silent.

"All right? Okay. We start there. You committed a vicious and mindless goddamned crime and I'm going to try and get you out of the consequences. But let's not clutter up the surface with a lot of horseshit about who stood by who and how you shouldn't tell secrets, and oh-of-course-anyone-would-have."

Susan said, between her teeth, "Spenser."

I drank some beer and ate a scallop. "Now start at the beginning and tell me everything that happened."

Pam Shepard said, "You will help me?"

"Yes."

She dried her eyes with her napkin. Snuffled a little. Susan gave her a Kleenex and she blew her nose. Delicately. My fisherman's platter had fried haddock in it. I pushed it aside, over behind the French fries, and ate a fried clam.

"Rose and Jane are organizing a women's movement. They feel we must overcome our own passivity and arouse our sisters to do the same. I think they want to model it on the Black Panthers, and to do that we need guns. Rose says we won't have to use them. But to have them will make a great psychological difference. It will increase the level of militancy and it will represent power, even, Jane says, a threat to phallic power."

"Phallic power?"

She nodded.

I said, "Go ahead."

"So they talked about it, and some other women came over and we had a meeting, and decided that we either had to steal the guns or the money to buy them. Jane had a gun, but that was all. Rose said it was easier to steal money than guns, and Jane said that it would be easy as pie to steal from a bank because banks always instruct their employees to cooperate with robbers anyway. What do they care, they are insured. And banks are where the money is. So that's where we should go."

I didn't say anything. Susan ate some crab salad. Pam Shepard seemed to have no interest in her lobster stew. Looked good too.

"So Rose and Jane said they would do the actual work," she

said. "And I — I don't know exactly why — I said I'd go with them. And Jane said that was terrific of me and proved that I was really into the women's movement. And Rose said a bank was the ideal symbol of masculine-capitalist oppression. And one of the other women, I don't know her name, she was a black woman, Cape Verdean I think, said that capitalism was itself masculine, and racist as well, so that the bank was a really perfect place to strike. And I said I wanted to go."

"Like an initiation," I said.

Susan nodded. Pam Shepard looked puzzled and shrugged. "Maybe, I don't know. Anyway we went and Jane and Rose and I all wore sunglasses and big hats. And Jane had the gun."

"Jane has all the fun," I said. Susan glared at me. Pam Shepard didn't seem to notice.

"Anyway, we went in and Rose and Jane went to the counter and I stayed by the door as a . . . a lookout . . . and Rose gave the girl, woman, behind the counter a note and Jane showed her the gun. And the woman did what it said. She took all her money from the cash drawer and put it in a bag that Rose gave her and we started to leave when that foolish old man tried to stop us. Why did he do that? What possessed him to take that chance?"

"Maybe he thought that was his job."

She shook her head. "Foolish old man. What is an old man like that working as a bank guard for anyway?"

"Probably a retired cop. Stood at an intersection for forty years and directed traffic and then retired and couldn't live on the pension. So he's got a gun and he hires out at the bank."

"But why try to stop us, an old man like that. I mean he saw Jane had a gun. It wasn't his money."

"Maybe he thought he ought to. Maybe he figured that if he were taking the money to guard the bank when the robbers didn't come, he ought to guard it when they did. Sort of a question of honor, maybe."

She shook her head. "Nonsense, that's the machismo convention. It gets people killed and for what. Life isn't a John Wayne movie."

"Yeah, maybe. But machismo didn't kill that old guy. Jane killed him."

"But she had to. She's fighting for a cause. For freedom. Not only for women but for men as well, freedom from all the old imperatives, freedom from the burden of machismo for you as well as for us."

"Right on," I said. "Off the bank guard."

Susan said, "What happened after Jane shot the guard?"

"We ran," Pam said. "Another woman, Grace something, I never knew her last name, was waiting for us in her Volkswagen station wagon, and we got in and drove back to the house."

"The one on Centre Street?" I asked.

She nodded. "And we decided there that we better split up. That we couldn't stay there because maybe they could identify us from the cameras. There were two in the bank that Rose spotted. I didn't know where to go so I went to the bus station in New Bedford and took the first bus going out, which was coming to Plymouth. The only time I'd ever been to Plymouth was when we took the kids to Plimoth Plantation when they were smaller. So I got off the bus and walked here. And then I didn't know what to do, so I sat in the snack bar at the reception center for a while and I counted what money I had, most of the hundred dollars you gave me, and I saw your card in my wallet and called you." She paused and stared out the window. "I almost called my husband. But that would have just been running home with my tail between my legs. And I started to call you and hung up a couple of times. I . . . Did I have to have a man to get me out of trouble? But then I had nowhere else to go and nothing else to try so I called." She kept looking out the window. The butter in her lobster stew was starting to form a skin as the stew cooled. "And after I called you I walked up and down the main street of the village and in and out of the houses and thought, here I am, forty-three years old and in the worst trouble of my life and I've got no one to call but a guy I've met once in my life, that I don't even know, no one else at all." She was crying now and her voice shook as she talked. She turned her head away further toward the window to hide it. The tide had gone out some more since I'd last looked and the dark water rounded rocks beyond the beach and made a kind of cobbled pattern with the sea breaking and foaming over them. It had gotten quite dark now, though it was early afternoon, and spits of rain splattered on the window. "And you think I'm a goddamned fool," she said. She had her hand on her mouth and it muffled her speech. "And I am."

Susan put her hand on Pam Shepard's shoulder. "I think I know how you feel," Susan said. "But it's the kind of thing he can do and others can't. You did what you felt you had to do, and you need help now, and you have the right person to help you. You did the right thing to call him. He can fix this. He doesn't think you are a fool. He's grouchy about other things, about me, and about himself, a lot of things and he leaned on you too hard. But he can help you with this. He can fix it."

"Can he make that old man alive again?"

"We don't work that way," I said. "We don't look around and see where we were. And we don't look down the road and see what's coming. We don't have anything to do but deal with what we know. We look at the facts and we don't speculate. We just keep looking right at this and we don't say what if, or I wish or if only. We just take it as it comes. First you need someplace to stay besides Plimoth Plantation. I'm not using my apartment because I'm down here working on things. So you can stay there. Come on, we'll go there now." I gestured for the check. "Suze," I said, "you and Pam go get in my car, I'll pay up here."

Pam Shepard said, "I have money."

I shook my head as the waitress came. Susan and Pam got up and went out. I paid the check, left a tip neither too big nor too small — I didn't want her to remember us — and went to the car after them.

15

IT'S FORTY-FIVE MINUTES from Plymouth to Boston and the traffic was light in midafternoon. We were on Marlborough Street in front of my apartment at three-fifteen. On the ride up Pam Shepard had given me nothing else I could use. She didn't know where Rose and Jane were. She didn't know how to find them. She didn't know who had the money, she assumed Rose. They had agreed, if they got separated, to put an ad in the New Bedford *Standard Times* personals column. She didn't know where Rose and Jane had expected to get the guns. She didn't know if they had any gun permit or FID card."

"Can't you just go someplace and buy them?" she said.

"Not in this state," I said.

She didn't know what kind of guns they had planned to buy. She didn't really know that guns came in various kinds. She didn't know anyone's name in the group except Rose and Jane and Grace and the only last name she knew was Alexander.

"It's a case I can really sink my teeth into," I said. "Lot of hard facts, lot of data. You're sure I've got your name right?"

She nodded.

"What's the wording for your ad," I said.

"If we get separated? We just say, 'Sisters, call me at' — then we give a phone number and sign our first name."

"And you run it in the *Standard Times?*"

"Yes, in the personal column."

We got out of the car and Pam said, "Oh, what a pretty location. There's the Common right down there."

"Actually the Public Garden. The Common's on the other side of Charles Street," I said. We went up to my apartment, second floor front. I opened the door.

Pam Shepard said, "Oh, very nice. Why it's as neat as a pin. I always pictured bachelor apartments with socks thrown around and whiskey bottles on the floor and wastebaskets spilling onto the floor."

"I have a cleaning person, comes in once a week."

"Very nice. Who did the woodcarvings?"

"I have a woodcarver come in once a week."

Susan said, "Don't listen to him. He does them."

"Isn't that interesting, and look at all the books. Have you read all these books?"

"Most of them, my lips get awful tired though. The kitchen is in here. There should be a fair supply of food laid in."

"And booze," Susan said.

"That too," I said. "In case the food runs out you can starve to death happy."

I opened the refrigerator and took out a bottle of Amstel. "Want a drink?" Both Susan and Pam said no. I opened the beer and drank some from the bottle.

"There's some bread and cheese and eggs in the refrigerator. There's quite a bit of meat in the freezer. It's labeled. And Syrian bread. There's coffee in the cupboard here." I opened the cupboard door. "Peanut butter, rice, canned tomatoes, flour, so forth. We can get you some vegetables and stuff later. You can make a list of what else you need."

I showed her the bathroom and the bedroom. "The sheets are clean," I said. "The person changes them each week, and she was here yesterday. You will need clothes and things." She nodded. "Why don't you make a list of food and clothes and toiletries and whatever that you need and Suze and I will go out and get them for you." I gave her a pad and pencil. She sat at the kitchen counter to write. While she did I talked at her. "When we leave," I said, "stay in here. Don't answer the door. I've got a key and Suze has a key and no one else has. So you won't have to open the door for us and no one else has reason to come here. Don't go out."

"What are you going to do?" she asked.

"I don't know," I said. "I'll have to think about it."

"I think maybe I'll have that drink you offered," she said.

"Okay, what would you like?"

"Scotch and water?"

"Sure."

I made her the drink, lots of ice, lots of Scotch, a dash of water. She sipped it while she finished her list.

When she gave it to me she also offered me her money.

"No," I said. "You may need it. I'll keep track of all this and when it's over I'll give you a bill."

She nodded. "If you want more Scotch," I said, "you know where it is."

Susan and I went out to shop. At the Prudential Center on Boylston Street we split up. I went into the Star Market for food and she went up to the shopping mall for clothes and toiletries. I was quicker with the food than she was with her part and I had to hang around for a while on the plaza by the funny statue of Atlas or Prometheus or whoever he was supposed to be. Across the way a movie house was running an action-packed double feature: *The Devil in Miss Jones* and *Deep Throat.* They don't make them like they used to. Whatever happened to Ken Maynard and his great horse, Tarzan? I looked some more at the statue. It looked like someone had done a takeoff on Michelangelo, and been taken seriously. Did Ken Maynard really have a great horse named Tarzan? If Ken were still working, his great horse would probably be named Bruce and be a leather freak. A young woman went by wearing a white T-shirt and no bra. On the T-shirt was stenciled TONY'S PX, GREAT FALLS, MONTANA. I was watching her walk away when Susan arrived with several ornate shopping bags.

"That a suspect?" Susan said.

"Remember I'm a licensed law officer. I was checking whether those cut-off Levis were of legal length."

"Were they?"

"I don't think so." I picked up my groceries and one of

Susan's shopping bags and we headed for the car. When we got home Pam Shepard was sitting by the front window looking out at Marlborough Street. She hadn't so far as I could see done anything else except perhaps freshen her drink. It was five o'clock and Susan agreed to join Pam for a drink while I made supper. I pounded some lamb steaks I'd bought for lamb cutlets. Dipped them in flour, then egg, then bread crumbs. When they were what Julia Child calls nicely coated I put them aside and peeled four potatoes. I cut them into little egg-shaped oblongs, which took a while, and started them cooking in a little oil, rolling them around to get them brown all over. I also started the cutlets in another pan. When the potatoes were evenly browned I covered them, turned down the heat and left them to cook through. When the cutlets had browned, I poured off the fat, added some Chablis and some fresh mint, covered them and let them cook. Susan came out into the kitchen once to make two new drinks. I made a Greek salad with feta cheese and ripe olives and Susan set the table while I took the lamb cutlets out of the pan and cooked down the wine. I shut off the heat, put in a lump of unsalted butter, swirled it through the wine essence and poured it over the cutlets. With the meal we had warm Syrian bread and most of a half gallon of California Burgundy. Pam Shepard told me it was excellent and what a good cook I was.

"I never liked it all that much," Pam said. "When I was a kid my mother never wanted me in the kitchen. She said I'd be messy. So when I got married I couldn't cook anything."

Susan said, "I couldn't cook, really, when I got married either."

"Harv taught me," Pam said. "I think he kind of liked to cook, but . . ." She shrugged. "That was the wife's job. So I did it. Funny how you cut yourself off from things you like because of . . . of nothing. Just convention, other people's assumptions about what you ought to be and do."

"Yet often they are our own assumptions, aren't they," Susan said. "I mean where do we get our assumptions about how things are or ought to be? How much is there really a discrete identifiable self trying to get out?" I drank some Burgundy.

"I'm not sure I follow," Pam said.

"It's the old controversy," Susan said. "Nature-nurture. Are you what you are because of genetics or because of environment? Do men make history or does history make men?"

Pam Shepard smiled briefly. "Oh yes, nature-nurture, Child Growth and Development, Ed. 103. I don't know, but I know I got shoved into a corner I didn't want to be in." She drank some of her wine, and held her glass toward the bottle. Not fully liberated. Fully liberated you pour the wine yourself. Or maybe the half-gallon bottle was too heavy. I filled her glass. She looked at the wine a minute. "So did Harvey," she said.

"Get shoved in a corner?" Susan said.

"Yes." She sipped at the wine. I did too. "He got shoved into the success corner."

"Money?" Susan asked.

"No, not really. Not money exactly. It was more being important, being a man that mattered, being a man that knew the score, knew what was happening. A mover and shaker. I don't think he cared all that much about the money, except it proved that he was on top. Does that make sense?" She looked at me.

"Yeah, like making the football team," I said. "I understand that."

"You ought to," Susan said.

Pam Shepard said, "Are you like that?"

I shrugged. Susan said, "Yes, he's like that. In a specialized way."

Pam Shepard said, "I would have thought he wasn't but I don't know him very well."

Susan smiled. "Well, he isn't exactly, but he is if that makes any sense."

I said, "What the hell am I, a pot roast, I sit here and you discuss me?"

Susan said, "I think you described yourself quite well this morning."

"Before or after you smothered me with passionate kisses?"

"Long before," she said.

"Oh," I said.

Pam Shepard said, "Well, why aren't you in the race? Why aren't you grunting and sweating to make the team, be a star, whatever the hell it is that Harvey and his friends are trying to do?"

"It's not easy to say. It's an embarrassing question because it requires me to start talking about integrity and self-respect and stuff you recently lumped under John Wayne movies. Like honor. I try to be honorable. I know that's embarrassing to hear. It's embarrassing to say. But I believe most of the nonsense that Thoreau was preaching. And I have spent a long time working on getting myself to where I could do it. Where I could live life largely on my own terms."

"Thoreau?" Pam Shepard said. "You really did read all those books, didn't you."

"And yet," Susan said, "you constantly get yourself involved in other lives and in other people's troubles. This is not Walden Pond you've withdrawn to."

I shrugged again. It was hard to say it all. "Everybody's got to do something," I said.

"But isn't what you do dangerous?" Pam Shepard said.

"Yeah, sometimes."

"He likes that part," Susan said. "He's very into tough. He won't admit it, maybe not even to himself, but half of what he's doing all the time is testing himself against other men. Proving how good he is. It's competition, like football."

"Is that so?" Pam Shepard said to me.

"Maybe. It goes with the job."

Susan said, "But you chose the job."

"It's a job that lets me choose," I said.

"And yet it cuts you off from a lot of things," Susan said. "You've cut yourself off from family, from home, from marriage."

"I don't know," I said. "Maybe."

"More than maybe," Susan said. "It's autonomy. You are the most autonomous person I've ever seen and you don't let anything into that. Sometimes I think the muscle you've built is like a shield, like armor, and you keep yourself private and alone inside there. The integrity complete, unviolated, impervious, safe even from love."

"We've gone some distance away from Harv Shepard, Suze,"

I said. I felt as if I'd been breathing shallow for a long time and needed a deep inhale.

"Not as far as it looks," Susan said. "One reason you're not into the corner that Pam's husband is in is because he took the chance. He married. He had kids. He took the risk of love and relationship and the risk of compromise that goes with it."

"But I don't think Harvey was working for us, Susan," Pam Shepard said.

"It's probably not that easy," I said. "It's probably not something you can cut up like that. Working for us, working for him."

"Well," Pam Shepard said, "there's certainly a difference."

"Sometimes I think there's never a difference and things never divide into column A and column B," I said. "Perhaps he had to be a certain kind of man for you, because he felt that was what you deserved. Perhaps to him it meant manhood, and perhaps he wanted to be a man for you."

Pam said, "Machismo again."

"Yeah, but machismo isn't another word for rape and murder. Machismo is really about honorable behavior."

"Then why does it lead so often to violence?"

"I don't know that it does, but if it does it might be because that's one of the places that you can be honorable."

"That's nonsense," Pam Shepard said.

"You can't be honorable when it's easy," I said. "Only when it's hard."

"When the going gets tough, the tough get going?" The scorn in Pam Shepard's voice had more body than the wine. "You sound like Nixon."

I did my David Frye impression. "I am not a crook," I said and looked shifty.

"Oh, hell, I don't know," she said. "I don't even know what we're talking about anymore. I just know it hasn't worked. None of it, not Harv, not the kids, not me, not the house and the business and the club and growing older, nothing."

"Yeah," I said, "but we're working on it, my love."

She nodded her head and began to cry.

16

I COULDN'T THINK of much to do about Pam Shepard crying so I cleared the table and hoped that Susan would come up with something. She didn't. And when we left, Pam Shepard was still snuffling and teary. It was nearly eleven and we were overfed and sleepy. Susan invited me up to Smithfield to spend the night and I accepted, quite graciously, I thought, considering the aggravation she'd been giving me.

"You haven't been slipping off to encounter groups under an assumed name, have you?" I said.

She shook her head. "I don't quite know why I'm so bitchy lately," she said.

"It's not bitchy, exactly. It's pushy. I feel from you a kind of steady pressure. An obligation to explain myself."

"And you don't like a pushy broad, right?"

"Don't start up again, and don't be so goddamned sensitive. You know I don't mean the cliché. If you think I worry about role reversal and who keeps in whose place, you've spent a lot of time paying no attention to me."

"True," she said. "I'm getting a little hyped about the whole subject."

"What whole subject? That's one of my problems. I think I know the rules of the game all right, but I don't know what the game is."

"Man-woman relationships, I guess."

"All of them or me and you."

"Both."

"Terrific, Suze, now we've got it narrowed down."

"Don't make fun. I think being middle-aged and female and single one must think about feminism, if you wish, women's rights and women vis-à-vis men. And of course that includes you and me. We care about each other, we see each other, we go on, but it doesn't develop. It seems directionless."

"You mean marriage?"

"I don't know. I don't think I mean just that. My god, am I still that conventional? I just know there's a feeling of incompleteness in us. Or, I suppose I can only speak for me, in me, and in the way I perceive our relationship."

"It ain't just wham-bam-thank-you-ma'am."

"No, I know that. That's not a relationship. I know I'm more than good tail. I know I matter to you. But . . ."

I paid my fifteen cents on the Mystic River Bridge and headed down its north slope, past the construction barricades that I think were installed when the bridge was built.

"I don't know what's wrong with me," she said.

"Maybe it's wrong with me," I said.

There weren't many cars on the Northeast Expressway at this time of night. There was a light fog and the headlights made a scalloped apron of light in front of us as we drove.

"Maybe," she said. Far right across the salt marshes the lights of the G.E. River Works gleamed. Commerce never rests.

"Explaining myself is not one of the things I do really well, like drinking beer, or taking a nap. Explaining myself is clumsy stuff. You really ought to watch what I do, and, pretty much, I think, you'll know what I am. Actually I always thought you knew what I am."

"I think I do. Much of it is very good, a lot of it is the best I've ever seen."

"Ah-ha," I said.

"I don't mean that," Susan said. The mercury arc lights at the newly renovated Saugus Circle made the wispy fog bluish and the Blue Star Bar look stark and unreal across Route 1.

"I know pretty well what you are," she said. "It's what we are that is bothersome. What the hell are we, Spenser?"

I swung off Route 1 at the Walnut Street exit and headed in toward Smithfield. "We're together," I said. "Why have we got to catalogue. Are we a couple? A pair? I don't know. You pick one."

"Are we lovers?"

On the right Hawkes Pond gleamed through a very thin fringe of trees. It was a long narrow pond and across it the land rose up in a wooded hill crowned with power lines. In the moonlight, with a wispy fog, it looked pretty good.

"Yeah," I said. "Yeah. We're lovers."

"For how long?" Susan said.

"For as long as we live," I said. "Or until you can't bear me anymore. Whichever comes first."

We were in Smithfield now, past the country club on the left, past the low reedy meadow that was a bird sanctuary, and the place where they used to have a cider mill, to Summer Street, almost to Smithfield Center. Almost to Susan's house.

"For as long as we live will come first," Susan said.

I drove past Smithfield Center with its old meeting house on the triangular common. A banner stretched across the street announced some kind of barbecue, I couldn't catch what in the dark. I put my hand out and Susan took it and we held hands to her house.

Everything was wet and glistening in the dark, picking up glints from the streetlights. It wasn't quite raining, but the fog was very damp and the dew was falling. Susan's house was a small cape, weathered shingles, flagstone walk, lots of shrubs. The front door was a Colonial red with small bull's-eye glass windows in the top. Susan unlocked it and went in. I followed her and shut the door. In the dark silent living room, I put my hands on Susan's shoulders and turned her slowly toward me, and put my arms around her. She put her face against my chest and we stood that way, wordless and still for a long time.

"For as long as we live," I said.

"Maybe longer," Susan said. There was an old steeple clock with brass works on the mantel in the living room and while I couldn't see it in the dark, I could hear it ticking loudly as we stood there pressed against each other. I thought about how nice Susan smelled, and about how strong her body felt, and about how difficult it is to say what you feel. And I said, "Come on, honey, let's go to bed." She didn't move, just pressed harder against me and I reached down with my left hand and scooped up her legs and carried her to the bedroom. I'd been there before and had no trouble in the dark.

17

IN THE MORNING, still damp from the shower, we headed back for the Cape, stopped on the way for steak and eggs in a diner and got to the hotel room I still owned about noon. The fog had lifted and the sun was as clean and bright as we were, though less splendidly dressed. In my mailbox was a note to call Harv Shepard.

I called him from my room while Susan changed into her bathing suit.

"Spenser," I said, "what do you want?"

"You gotta help me."

"That's what I was telling you just a little while back," I said.

"I gotta see you, it's, it's outta control. I can't handle it. I need help. That, that goddamned nigger shoved one of my kids. I need help."

"Okay," I said. "I'll come over."

"No," he said. "I don't want you here. I'll come there. You in the hotel?"

"Yep." I gave him my room number. "I'll wait for you."

Susan was wiggling her way into a one-piece bathing suit. "Anything?" she said.

"Yeah, Shepard's coming apart. I guess Hawk made a move at one of the kids and Shepard's in a panic. He's coming over."

"Hawk scares me," Susan said. She slipped her arms through the shoulder straps.

"He scares me too, my love."

"He's . . ." She shrugged. "Don't go against him."

"Better me than Shepard," I said.

"Why better you than Shepard?"

"Because I got a chance and Shepard has none."

"Why not the police?"

"We'll have to ask Shepard that. Police are okay by me. I got no special interest in playing Russian roulette with Hawk. Shepard called him a nigger."

Susan shrugged. "What's that got to do?"

"I don't know," I said. "But I wish he hadn't done that. It's insulting."

"My God, Spenser, Hawk has threatened this man's life, beaten him up, abused his children, and you're worried about a racial slur?"

"Hawk's kind of different," I said.

She shook her head. "So the hell are you," she said. "I'm off to the pool to work on my tan. When you get through you can join me there. Unless you decide to elope with Hawk."

"Miscegenation," I said. "Frightful."

She left. About two minutes later Shepard arrived. He was moving better now. Some of the stiffness had gone from his walk, but confidence had not replaced it. He had on a western-cut, black-checked leisure suit and a white shirt with black stitching, the collar out over the lapels of the suit. There was a high shine on his black-tasseled loafers and his face was gray with fear.

"You got a drink here," he said.

"No, but I'll get one. What do you like?"

"Bourbon."

I called room service and ordered bourbon and ice. Shepard walked across the room and stared out the window at the golf course. He sat down in the armchair by the window and got right up again. "Spenser," he said. "I'm scared shit."

"I don't blame you," I said.

"I never thought . . . I always thought I could handle business, you know? I mean I'm a businessman and a businessman is supposed to be able to handle business. I'm supposed to know how to put a deal together and how to make it work. I'm supposed to be able to manage people. But this. I'm no goddamned candy-ass. I been around and all, but these people . . ."

"I know about these people."

"I mean that goddamned nigger . . ."

"His name's Hawk," I said. "Call him Hawk."

"What are you, the NAACP?"

"Call him Hawk."

"Yeah, okay, Hawk. My youngest came in the room while they were talking to me and Hawk grabbed him by the shirt and put him out the door. Right in front of me. The black bastard."

"Who are they?"

"They?"

"You said your kid came in while they were talking to you."

"Oh, yeah." Shepard walked back to the window and looked out again. "Hawk and a guy named Powers. White guy. I guess Hawk works for him."

"Yeah, I know Powers."

The room service waiter came with the booze on a tray. I signed the check and tipped him a buck. Shepard rummaged in his pocket. "Hey, let me get that," he said.

"I'll put it on your bill," I said. "What did Powers want? No, better, I'll tell you what he wanted. You owe him money and you can't pay him and he's going to let you off the hook a little if you let him into your business a lot."

"Yeah." Shepard poured a big shot over ice from the bottle of bourbon and slurped at it. "How the hell did you know?"

"Like I said, I know Powers. It's also not a very new idea. Powers and a lot of guys like him have done it before. A guy like you mismanages the money, or sees a chance for a big break or overextends himself at the wrong time and can't get financing. Powers comes along, gives you the break, charges an exorbitant weekly interest. You can't pay, he sends Hawk around to convince you it's serious. You still can't pay so Powers comes around and says you can give me part of the business or you can cha-cha once more with Hawk. You're lucky, you got me to run to. Most guys got no one but the cops."

"I didn't mismanage the money."

"Yeah, course not. Why not go to the cops?"

"No cops," Shepard said. He drank some more bourbon.

"Why not?"

"They'll start wanting to know why I needed money from Powers."

"And you were cutting a few corners?"

"Goddamnit, I had to. Everybody cuts a few corners."

"Tell me about the ones you cut."

"Why? What do you need to know that for?"

"I won't know till you tell me."

Shepard drank some more bourbon. "I was in a box. I had to do something." The drape on the right side of the window hung crookedly. Shepard straightened it. I waited. "I was in business with an outfit called Estate Management Corporation. They go around to different vacation-type areas and develop leisure homes in conjunction with a local guy. Around here I was the local guy. What we did was set up a separate company with me as president. I did the developing, dealt with the town planning board, building inspector, that stuff, and supervised the actual construction. They provided architects, planners and financing and the sales force. It's a little more complicated than that, but you get the idea. My company was a wholly owned subsidiary of Estate Management. You follow that okay?"

"Yeah. I got that. I'm not a shrewd-o business tycoon like you, but if you talk slowly and I can watch your lips move, I can keep up, I think. What was the name of your company?"

"We called the development Promised Land. And the company was Promised Land, Inc."

"Promised Land." I whistled. "Cu-ute," I said. "Were you aiming at an exclusive Jewish clientele?"

"Huh? Jewish? Why Jewish? Anybody was welcome. I mean we wouldn't be thrilled if the Shvartzes moved in maybe, but we didn't care about religion."

I wished I hadn't said it. "Okay," I said. "So you're president of Promised Land, Inc., a wholly owned subsidiary of Estate Management, Inc. Then what?"

"Estate Management went under."

"Bankrupt?"

"Yeah." Shepard emptied his bourbon and I poured some more in the glass. I offered ice and he shook his head. "The way it worked was the Estate Management people would see the land, really high-powered stuff, contact people, closers, free trips to Florida, the whole bag. The buyer would put a deposit on the land and would also sign a contract for the kind of house he wanted. We had about six models to choose from. He'd put a deposit on the house as well, and that deposit would go into an escrow account."

"What happened to the land deposit?"

"Went to Estate Management."

"Okay, and who controlled the house escrow?"

Shepard said, "Me."

"And when Estate Management pulled out, and you were stuck with a lot of money invested and no backing, you dipped into the escrow."

"Yeah, I used it all. I had to. When Estate Management folded, the town held up on the building permits. All there was was the building sites staked off. We hadn't brought the utilities in yet. You know, water, sewage, that kind of thing."

I nodded.

"Well, the town said, nobody gets a permit to build anything until the utilities are in. They really screwed me. I mean, I guess they had to. Things smelled awful funny when Estate went bankrupt. A lot of money disappeared, all those land deposits, and a lot of people started wondering about what happened. It smelled awful bad. But I was humped. I had all my capital tied up in the goddamned land and the only way I was going to get it back was to build the houses and sell them. But I couldn't do that because I couldn't get a permit until I put in the utilities. And I couldn't put in the utilities because I didn't have any money. And nobody wanted to finance the thing. Banks only want to give you money when you can prove you don't need it, you know that. And they really didn't want to have anything to do with Promised Land, because by now the story was all around financial circles and the IRS and the SEC and the Mass attorney general's office and the FCC and a bunch of other people were starting to investigate Estate Management, and a group of people who'd bought land were suing Estate Management. So I scooped the escrow money. I was stuck. It was that or close up shop and start looking for work without enough money to have my résumé typed. I'm forty-five years old."

"Yeah, I know. Let me guess the next thing that happened. The group that was suing Estate Management also decided to get its house deposit back."

Shepard nodded.

"And of course, since you'd used it to start bringing in utilities, you couldn't give it back."

He kept nodding as I talked.

"So you found Powers someplace and he lent you the dough. What was the interest rate? Three percent a week?"

"Three and a half."

"And, of course, payment on the principal."

Shepard nodded some more.

"And you couldn't make it."

Nod.

"And Hawk beat you up."

"Yeah. Actually he didn't do it himself. He had two guys do it, and he, like, supervised."

"Hawk's moving up. Executive level. He was always a comer."

"He said he just does the killing now, the sweaty work he delegates."

"And so here we are."

"Yeah," Shepard said. He leaned his head against the window. "The thing is, Powers' money bailed me out. I was coming back. The only money I owe is Powers and I can't pay. It's like — I'm so close and the only way to win is to lose."

18

SHEPARD LOOKED at me expectantly when he was through telling me his sins.

"What do you want," I said, "absolution? Say two Our Fathers and three Hail Marys and make a good act of contrition? Confession may be good for the soul but it's not going to help your body any if we can't figure a way out."

"What could I do," he said. "I was in a corner, I had to crib on the escrow money. Estate Management got off with four or five million bucks. Was I supposed to watch it all go down the pipe? Everything I've been working for? Everything I am?"

"Someday we can talk about just what the hell you were working for, and maybe even what you are. Not now. How hot is Powers breathing on your neck?"

"We've got a meeting set up for tomorrow."

"Where?"

"At Hawk's room in the Holiday Inn."

"Okay, I'll go with you."

"What are you going to do?"

"I don't know. I've got to think. But it's better than going alone, isn't it."

Shepard's breath came out in a rush. "Oh, hell, yes," he said, and finished the bourbon.

"Maybe we can talk them into an extension," I said. "The more time I got, the more chance to work out something."

"But what can we do?"

"I don't know. What Powers is doing, remember, is illegal. If we get really stuck we can blow the whistle and you can be state's evidence against Powers and get out of it with a tongue-lashing."

"But I'm ruined."

"Depends how you define ruined," I said. "Being King Powers' partner, rich or poor, would be awful close to ruination. Being dead also."

"No," he said. "I can't go to the cops."

"Not yet you can't. Maybe later you'll have to."

"How would I get Pam back? Broke, no business, my name in the papers for being a goddamned crook? You think she'd come back and live with me in a four-room cottage while I collected welfare?"

"I don't know. She doesn't seem to be coming back to you while, as far as she knows, you're up on top."

"You don't know her. She's always watching. Who's got how much, who's house is better or worse than ours, who's lawn is greener or browner. You don't know her."

"She's another problem," I said. "We'll work on her too, but we can't get into marriage encounter until this problem is solved."

"Yeah, but just remember, what I told you is absolutely confidential. I can't risk everything. There's got to be another way."

"Harv," I said. "You're acting like you got lots of options. You don't. You reduced your options when you dipped into the escrow, and you goddamned near eliminated them when you took some of Powers' money. We're talking about people who might shoot you. Remember that."

Shepard nodded. "There's got to be a way."

"Yeah, there probably is. Let me think about it. What time's the meeting tomorrow?"

"One o'clock."

"I'll pick you up at your house about twelve forty-five. Go home, stay there. If I need you I want to be able to reach you."

"What are you going to do?"

"I'm going to think."

Shepard left. Half sloshed and a little relieved. Talking about a

problem sometimes gives you the illusion you've done something about it. At least he wasn't trying to handle it alone. Nice
clientele I had. The cops wanted Pam and the crooks wanted
Harv.

I went out to the pool. Susan was sitting in a chaise in
her red-flowered one-piece suit reading *The Children of the
Dream*, by Bruno Bettelheim. She had on big, gold-rimmed
sunglasses and a large white straw hat with a red band that
matched the bathing suit. I stopped before she saw me and
looked at her. Jesus Christ, I thought. How could anyone have
ever divorced her? Maybe she'd divorced him. We'd never
really talked much about it. But even so, where was he? If she'd
divorced me, I'd have followed her around for the rest of our
lives. I walked over, put my arms on either side of her and
did a push-up on the chaise. Lowering myself until our noses
touched.

"If you and I were married, and you divorced me, I would
follow you around the rest of my life," I said.

"No you wouldn't," she said. "You'd be too proud."

"I would assault anyone you dated."

"That I believe. But you're not married to me and get off of
me, you goof. You're just showing off."

I did five or six push-ups over her on the chaise.

"Why do you say that?" I said.

She poked me with her index finger in the solar plexus. "Off,"
she said.

I did one more push-up. "You know what this makes me think
of?"

"Of course I know what it makes you think of. Now get the
hell off me, you're bending my book."

I snapped off one more push-up and bounced off the chaise the
way a gymnast dismounts the parallel bars. Straightening to
attention as my feet hit.

"Once you put adolescence behind you," Susan said, "you'll
be quite an attractive guy, a bit physical but . . . attractive. What
did Shepard want?"

"Help," I said. "He's into a loan shark as we assumed, and the
loan shark wants his business." I got a folding chair from across

the pool and brought it back and sat beside Susan and told her about Shepard and his problem.

"That means you are going to have to deal with Hawk," Susan said.

"Maybe," I said.

She clamped her mouth in a thin line and took a deep breath through her nose. "What are you going to do?"

"I don't know. I thought I'd go down and sit in the bar and think. Want to come?"

She shook her head. "No, I'll stay here and read and maybe swim in a while. When you think of something, let me know. We can have lunch or something to celebrate."

I leaned over and kissed her on the shoulder, and went to the bar. There were people having lunch, but not many drinking. I sat at the far end of the bar, ordered a Harp on draft and started in on the peanuts in the dark wooden bowl in front of me.

I had two problems. I had to take King Powers off of Shepard's back and I had to get Pam Shepard off the hook for armed robbery and murder. Saps. I was disgusted with both of them. It's an occupational hazard, I thought. Everyone gets contemptuous after a while of his clients. Teachers get scornful of students, doctors of patients, bartenders of drinkers, salesmen of buyers, clerks of customers. But, Jesus, they were saps. The Promised Land. Holy Christ. I had another beer. The peanut bowl was empty. I rattled it on the bar until the bartender came down and refilled it. Scornfully, I thought. Guns, I thought. Get guns and disarm phallic power. Where the hell were they going to get guns? They could look in the yellow pages under gunrunner. I could put them in touch with somebody like King Powers. Then when he sold them the guns they could shoot him and that would solve Shepard's problem . . . Or I could frame Powers. No, frame wasn't right. Entrapment. That's the word. I could entrap Powers. Not for sharking: That would get Shepard in the soup too. But for illegal gun sales. Done right it would get him off Shepard's back for quite a long time. It would also get Rose and Jane out of Pam Shepard's life. But why wouldn't they take Pam down with them? Because I could deal with the local D.A.: Powers and two radical feminists on a fresh roll, if he kept the Shepards out of it. I liked it. It needed a little more shape and substance. But I liked it. It could work. My only other idea was appealing to Powers' better instincts. That didn't hold much promise. Entrapment was better. I was going to flimflam the old King. A little Scott Joplin music in the background, maybe. I had another beer and ate more peanuts and thought some more.

Susan came in from the pool with a thigh-length white lace thing over her bathing suit, and slid onto the barstool next to me.

"Cogito ergo sum," I said.

"Oh absolutely," she said. "You've always been sicklied over with the pale cast of thought."

"Wait'll you hear," I said.

19

AFTER LUNCH I called the New Bedford *Standard Times* and inserted an ad in the personals column of the classified section: "Sisters, call me at 936-1434. Pam."

Then I called 936-1434. Pam Shepard answered the first ring.

"Listen," I said. And read her the ad. "I just put that in the New Bedford *Standard Times*. When the sisters call you arrange for us to meet. You, me, them."

"Oh, they won't like that. They won't trust you."

"You'll have to get them to do it anyway. Talk to them of obligation and sororal affiliation. Tell them I've got a gun dealer who wants to talk. How you get us together is up to you, but do it."

"Why is it so important?"

"To save your hide and Harv's and make the world safe for democracy. Just do it. It's too complicated to explain. You getting stir-crazy there?"

"No, it's not too bad. I've seen a lot of daytime television."

"Don't watch too much, it'll rot your teeth."

"Spenser?"

"Yeah."

"What's wrong with Harvey? What did you mean about saving Harvey's hide?"

"Nothing you need worry about now. I'm just concerned with his value system."

"He's all right?"

"Sure."

"And the kids?"

"Of course. They miss you, Harv, too, but they're fine otherwise." Ah, Spenser, you glib devil you. How the hell did I know how they were? I'd seen one of them my first day on the case.

"Funny," she said. "I don't know if I miss them or not, sometimes I think I do, but sometimes I just think I ought to and am feeling guilty because I don't. It's hard to get in touch with your feelings sometimes."

"Yeah, it is. Anything you need right now before I hang?"

"No, no thanks, I'm okay."

"Good. Suze or I will be in touch."

I hung up.

Susan in faded Levis and a dark blue blouse was heading down Cape to look at antiques. "And I may pick up some young stud still in college and fulfill my wildest fantasies," she said.

I said, "Grrrrrr."

"Women my age are at the peak of their erotic power," she said. "Men your age are in steep decline."

"I'm young at heart," I said. Susan was out the door. She stuck her head back in. "I wasn't talking about heart," she said. And went. I looked at my watch. It was one-fifteen. I went in the bathroom, splashed some water on my face, toweled dry and headed for New Bedford.

At five after two I was illegally parked outside the New Bedford Police Station on Spring Street. It was three stories, brick, with A dormers on the roof and a kind of cream yellow trim. Flanking the entrance, just like in the Bowery Boys movies, were white globes on black iron columns. On the globes it said NEW BEDFORD POLICE in black letters. A couple of tan police cruisers with blue shields on the door were parked out front. One of them was occupied, and I noticed that the New Bedford cops wore white hats. I wondered if the crooks wore black ones.

At the desk I asked a woman cop who was handling the Bristol Security robbery. She had light hair and blue eyeshadow and shiny lipstick and she looked at me hard for about ten seconds. "Who wants to know?" she said.

Not sex nor age nor national origin makes any difference. Cops are cops.

"My name's Spenser," I said. "I'm a private license from Boston and I have some information that's going to get someone promoted to sergeant."

"I'll bet you do," she said. "Why don't you lay a little on me and see if I'm impressed."

"You on the case?"

"I'm on the desk, but impress me anyway."

I shook my head. "Detectives," I said, "I only deal with detectives."

"Everybody only deals with detectives. Every day I sit here with my butt getting wider, and every day guys like you come in and want to talk with a detective." She picked up the phone on the desk, dialed a four-digit number and said into the mouthpiece, "Sylvia there? Margaret on the desk. Yeah. Well, tell him there's a guy down here says he's got information on Bristol Security. Okay." She hung up. "Guy in charge is a detective named Jackie Sylvia. Sit over there, he'll be down in a minute."

It was more like five before he showed up. A squat bald man with dark skin. He was as dapper as a guy can be who stands five-six and weighs two hundred. Pink-flowered shirt, a beige leisure suit, coppery brown patent leather loafers with a couple of bright gold links on the tops. It was hard to tell how old he was. His round face was without lines, but the close-cropped hair that remained below his glistening bald spot was mostly gray. He walked over to me with a light step and I suspected he might not be as fat as he looked.

"My name's Sylvia," he said. "You looking for me?"

"I am if you're running the Bristol Security investigation."

"Yeah."

"Can we go someplace and talk?"

Sylvia nodded toward the stairs past the desk and I followed him to the second floor. We went through a door marked ROBBERY and into a room that overlooked Second Street. There were six desks butted together in groups of two, each with a push-button phone and a light maple swivel chair. In the far corner an office had been partitioned off. On the door was a sign that read SGT. CRUZ. At one of the desks a skinny cop with scraggly blond hair sat with his feet up talking on the phone. He was wearing a black T-shirt, and on his right forearm he had a tattoo of a thunderbird and the words FIGHTING 45TH. A cigarette burned on the edge of the desk, a long ash forming. Sylvia grabbed a straight chair from beside one of the other desks and dragged it over beside his. "Sit," he said. I sat and he slid into his swivel chair and tilted it back, his small feet resting on the base of the chair. He wasn't wearing socks. A big floor fan in the far corner moved hot air back and forth across the desk tops as it scanned the room.

On Sylvia's desk was a paper coffee cup, empty, and part of a peanut butter sandwich on white bread. "Okay," Sylvia said. "Shoot."

"You know who King Powers is?" I said.

"Yeah."

"I can give you the people who did the Bristol Security and I can give you Powers, but there's got to be a trade."

"Powers don't do banks."

"I know. I can give him to you for something else, and I can give you the bank people and I can tie them together, but I gotta have something back from you."

"What do you want?"

"I want two people who are in this, left out of this."

"One of them you?"

"No, I don't do banks either."

"Let me see something that tells me what you do do."

I showed him my license. He looked at it, handed it back. "Boston, huh. You know a guy named Abel Markum up there, works out of Robbery?"

"Nope."

"Who do you know?"

"I know a homicide lieutenant named Quirk. A dick named Frank Belson. Guy in Robbery named Herschel Patton. And I have a friend that's a school-crossing guard in Billerica named . . ."

Sylvia cut me off. "Okay, okay, I done business with Patton." He took some grape-flavored sugarless bubble gum from his shirt pocket and put two pieces in his mouth. He didn't offer any to me. "You know, if you're in possession of evidence of the commission of a felony that you have no legal right to withhold that evidence."

"Can I have a piece of bubble gum?"

Sylvia reached into his pocket, took out the pack and tossed it on the desk in front of me. There were three pieces left. I took one.

"Take at least two," Sylvia said. "You can't work up a bubble with one. Stuffs lousy."

I took another piece, peeled off the paper and chewed it. Sylvia was right. It was lousy.

"Remember when Double Bubble used to put out the nice lump of pink bubble gum and it was all you needed to get a good bubble?"

"Times change," Sylvia said. "Withholding information of a felony is illegal."

I blew a small purple bubble. "Yeah, I know. You want to talk about trade?"

"How about we slap you in a cell for a while as an accessory to a felony?"

I worked on the bubble gum. It wasn't elastic enough. I could only produce a small bubble, maybe as big as a Ping-Pong ball, before it broke with a sharp little snap.

"How about while you're in the cell we interrogate you a while. We got some guys down here can interrogate the shit out of a person. You know?"

"This stuff sticks to your teeth," I said.

"Not if you don't have any," Sylvia said.

"Why the hell would someone make gum that sticks to your teeth," I said. "Christ, you can't trust anyone."

"You don't like it, spit it out. I don't make you chew it."

"It's better than nothing," I said.

"You gonna talk to me about the Bristol Security job?"

"I'm gonna talk to you about a trade."

"Goddamnit, Spenser, you can't come waltzing in here and tell me what kind of deal you'll make with me. I don't know what kind of crap you get away with up in Boston, but down here I tell you what kind of deal there is."

"Very good," I said. "One look at my license and you

remembered my name. I didn't even see your lips move when you looked at it either."

"Don't smart-ass with me, Johnny, or you'll be looking very close at the floor. Understand what I'm saying to you?"

"Aw come on, Sylvia, stop terrifying me. When I get panicky I tend to violence and there's only two of you in the room." The scraggly haired cop with the tattoo had hung up the phone and drifted over to listen.

"Want me to open the window, Jackie," he said. "Then if he gets mean we can scream for help?"

"Or jump," Sylvia said. "It's two floors but it would be better than trying to deal with an animal like this."

I said, "You guys want to talk trade yet, or are you working up a nightclub act?"

"How do I know you can deliver," Sylvia said.

"If I don't, what have you lost. You're no worse off than you are now."

"No entrapment," scraggly hair said. "At least nothing that looks like entrapment in court. We been burned on that a couple of times."

"No sweat," I said.

"How bad are the people you want left out?"

"They are no harm to anybody but themselves," I said. "They ran after the wrong promise and got into things they couldn't control."

"The bank guard that got killed," Sylvia said, "I knew him. Used to be in the department here, you know."

"I know," I said. "My people didn't want it to happen."

"Homicide during the commission of a felony is murder one."

"I know that too," I said. "And I know that these people are a good swap for what I can give you. Somebody's got to go down for the bank guard."

Sylvia interrupted. "Fitzgerald, his name was. Everybody called him Fitzy."

"Like I say, somebody has to go down for that. And somebody will. I just want to save a couple of goddamned fools."

Scraggly hair looked at Sylvia. "So far we got zip on the thing, Jackie. Air."

"You got a plan," Sylvia said.

I nodded.

"There's no guarantee. Whatever you got, I'm going to have to check you out first."

"I know that."

"Okay, tell me."

"I thought you'd never ask," I said.

20

SCRAGGLY HAIR'S name turned out to be McDermott. He and Jackie Sylvia listened without comment while I laid it out and when I was through Sylvia said, "Okay, we'll think about it. Where can I reach you?"

"Dunfey's in Hyannis. Or my service if I'm not there. I check with the service every day." I gave him the number.

"We'll get back to you."

On the drive back to Hyannis the grape bubble gum got harder and harder to chew. I gave up in Wareham and spit it out the window in front of the hospital. The muscles at my jaw hinges were sore, and I felt slightly nauseous. When I pulled into the parking lot at Dunfey's it was suppertime and the nausea had given way to hunger.

Susan was back from her antiquing foray and had a Tiffany-style glass lampshade for which she'd paid $125. We went down to the dining room, had two vodka gimlets each, parslied rack of lamb and blackberry cheesecake. After dinner we had some cassis and then went down to the ballroom and danced all the slow numbers until midnight. We brought a bottle of champagne back to the room and drank it and went to bed and didn't sleep until nearly three.

It was ten-forty when I woke up. Susan was still asleep, her back to me, the covers up tight around her neck. I picked up the phone and ordered breakfast, softly. "Don't knock," I said. "Just leave it outside the door. My friend is still asleep."

I showered and shaved and with a towel around my waist opened the door and brought in the cart. I drank coffee and ate from a basket of assorted muffins while I dressed. Susan woke up as I was slipping my gun into the hip holster. I clipped the holster on to my belt. She lay on her back with her hands behind her head and watched me. I slipped on my summer blazer with the brass buttoms and adjusted my shirt collar so it rolled out nicely over the lapels. Seductive.

"You going to see Hawk and what's'isname?" Susan said.

"Powers," I said. "Yeah. Me and Harv Shepard."

She continued to look at me.

"Want some coffee?" I said.

She shook her head. "Not yet."

I ate a corn muffin.

"Are you scared?" Susan asked.

"I don't know. I don't think much about it. I don't see anything very scary happening today."

"Do you like it?"

"Yeah. I wouldn't do it if I didn't like it."

"I mean this particularly. I know you like the work. But do you like this? You are going to frame a very dangerous man. That should scare you, or excite you or something."

"I'm not going to frame him. I'm going to entrap him, in fact."

"You know what I mean. If it doesn't work right he'll kill you."

"No, he'll have it done."

"Don't do that. Don't pick up the less important part of what I'm saying. You know what I'm after. What kind of man does the kinds of things you do? What kind of man gets up in the morning and showers and shaves and checks the cartridges in his gun?"

"Couldn't we talk over the transports of delight in which we soared last evening?"

"Do you laugh at everything?"

"No, but we're spending too much time on this kind of talk. The kind of man I am is not a suitable topic, you know. It's not what one talks about."

"Why?"

"Because it's not."

"The code? A man doesn't succumb to self-analysis? It's weak? It's womanish?"

"It's pointless. What I am is what I do. Finding the right words for it is no improvement. It isn't important whether I'm scared or excited. It's important whether or not I do it. It doesn't matter to Shepard why. It matters to Shepard if."

"You're wrong. It matters more than that. It matters why."

"Maybe it matters mostly how."

"My, aren't we epigrammatic. Spencer Tracy and Katharine Hepburn. Repartee."

"He spells his name differently," I said.

Susan turned over on her side, her back to me, and was quiet. I had some more coffee. The murmurous rush of the air conditioner seemed quite loud. I'd asked for the New Bedford *Standard Times* with breakfast, and in the quiet, I picked it up and turned to the classified section. My ad was there under personals. "Sisters, call me at 936-1434. Pam." I looked at the sports page and finished my coffee. It was ten after twelve. I folded the paper and put it on the room service cart.

"Gotta go, Suze," I said.

She nodded without turning over.

I got up, put on my sunglasses and opened the door. "Spenser," she said, "I don't want us to be mad at each other."

"Me either," I said. I still had hold of the doorknob.

"Come back when you can," she said. "I miss you when you're gone."

"Me too," I said. I left the door open and went back and kissed her on the cheekbone, up near the temple. She rolled over on her back and looked up at me. Her eyes were wet. "Bye-bye," I said.

"Bye-bye."

I went out and closed the door and headed for Harv Shepard's place with my stomach feeling odd.

I don't know if I was scared or not, but Shepard was so scared his face didn't fit. The skin was stretched much too tight over the bones and he swallowed a lot, and loudly, as we drove out Main Street to the Holiday Inn.

"You don't need to know what I'm up to," I said. "I think you'll do better if you don't. Just take it that I've got something working that might get you out of this."

"Why can't you tell me?"

"Because it requires some deception and I don't think you're up to it."

"You're probably right," he said.

Hawk had a room on the second floor, overlooking the pool. He answered the door when we knocked, and Shepard and I went in. There was assorted booze on the bureau to the right, and a thin guy with horn-rimmed glasses reading the *Wall Street Journal* on one of the beds. King Powers was sitting at a round table with an open ledger in front of him, his hands folded on the edge of the table. Stagy bastard.

"What is that you have with you," Powers said in a flat Rudy Vallee voice.

"We're friends," I said. "We go everywhere together."

Powers was a tall, soft-looking man with pale skin and reddish hair trimmed long like a Dutch boy, and augmented with fuzzy mutton-chop sideburns. His wardrobe looked like Robert Hall Mod. Maroon-checked double-knit leisure suit, white belt, white shoes, white silk shirt with the collar out over the lapels. A turquoise arrowhead was fastened around his neck on a leather thong and stuck straight out, like a gesture of derision.

"I didn't tell you to bring no friends," Powers said to Shepard.

"You'll be glad he did," I said. "I got a package for you that will put a lot of change in your purse."

"I don't use no goddamned purse," Powers said.

"Oh," I said. "I'm sorry. I thought that was your mistress on the bed."

Behind me Hawk murmured, "Hot damn" to himself. The guy on the bed looked up from his *Wall Street Journal* and frowned.

Powers said, "Hawk, get him the fuck out of here."

Hawk said, "This is Spenser. I told you about him. He likes to kid around but he don't mean harm. Leastwise he don't always mean harm."

"Hawk, you hear me. I told you move him out."

"He talking money, King. Maybe you should listen."

"You working for me, Hawk? You do what you're told."

"Naw. I only do what I want. I never do what I'm told. Same with old Spenser here. You yell your ass off at him, if you want, but he ain't going to do a goddamned thing he don't want to do. You and Macey listen to him. He talking about money, he probably ain't bullshitting. You don't like what you hear. Then I'll move him out."

"Aw right, aw right. Let's hear it, for crissake. Spit it out." Powers' pale face was a little red and he was looking at me hard. Macey, on the bed, had sat up, and put his feet on the floor. He still held the *Journal* in his left hand, his forefinger keeping the place.

"Okay, King. First. Harv can't pay up, at this time."

"Then his ass is grass and I'm a fucking lawnmower," Powers said.

"Trendy," I said.

"Huh?"

"Trendy as a bastard, that slick maroon and white combo. And to top it off you talk so good. You're just an altogether with-it guy."

"You keep fucking around with me, Spenser, and you're going to wish you never did."

"Whyn't you get to the part about the bread, Spenser," Hawk said. "In the purse. Whyn't you talk on that."

"I got a buyer with about a hundred thousand dollars who is looking for some guns. I will trade you the buyer for Shepard."

"What makes you think I can get guns?"

"King, for a hundred thousand skins you could get a dancing aardvark," I said.

He smiled. His lips were puffy and when he smiled the inside of his upper lip turned out. And his gums showed above his top teeth.

"Yeah, maybe I could," he said. "But Shepard's into me for a lot of fucking dough." He ran his eyes down the ledger page in front of him. "Thirty big ones. I took a lot of risk with that dough, just on a handshake, you know? It ain't easy to trade that off."

"Okay," I said. "See you, we'll take it elsewhere," I said. "Come on, Harv."

Powers said, "You're choice, but your pal better have the payment on him now, or we're going to be awful mad."

"The payment's in the offer. You turned it down, you got no bitch." I turned to go. Hawk was between us and the door. His hands resting delicately on his hips.

"Hawk," Powers said. "Shepard don't leave."

"Hundred thousand's a lotta vegetable matter, King," Hawk said.

"Hawk's right, Mr. Powers." Macey on the bed had dropped his *Journal* and brought out a neat-looking little .25 automatic with a pearl handle and nickel plating. Probably matched his cuff links.

"What's in it for you, Spenser?" Powers said.

"Thirty percent," I said. "You can use it to pay off Shepard's loan."

Powers was quiet. We all were. It was like a stop frame in instant replay.

Hawk at ease in front of the door. Shepard with his skin squeezing tight on his body, Macey with his cute gun. Powers sitting at the table, thinking.

The window was behind him and the light coming in framed him like a back-lit photograph. The little tendrils of fuzz in the double-knit were silhouetted and clear along his coat sleeves and the tops of the shoulders. The mutton-chop sideburns where the whiskers individuated at the outer edge were more gold than copper against the light.

"Who's your customer?" King said. Hawk whistled shave-and-a-haircut-two-bits between his teeth. Softly.

"If I told you that I probably wouldn't be needed as go-between, would I?"

Powers turned his lip up again and giggled. Then he turned to the thin guy. "Macey," he said, "I got some golf to play. Set this thing up." He looked at me. "This better be straight," he said. "If it ain't you are going to be pushing up your fucking daisies. You unnerstand? Fucking daisies you'll be pushing up." He got up and walked past me toward the door.

"Daisies," I said.

He went out. Macey put the .25 away and said, "Okay, let's get to work."

I said, "Is he going to play golf in his Anderson-Little cutaway?"

"He's going to change in the clubhouse," Macey said. "Haven't you ever played golf?"

"Naw, we were into aggravated assault when I was a kid."

Macey smiled once, on and off like a blinking light. Hawk went and lay down on the bed and closed his eyes. Shepard went stiffly to the bureau where the booze was and made a big drink. Macey sat down at the round table and I joined him. "Okay," he said, "give me the deal."

21

THERE WASN'T ALL that much to set up with Macey yet. I told him I'd have to get in touch with the other principals first and get back to him, but that the 100 grand was firm and he should start getting in touch with his sources.

"The guns would be top dollar," Macey said. "There's the risk factor, and the added problem of market impact. Large quantity like this causes ripples, as you must know."

"I know. And I know you can manage it. That's why I came to you."

Macey said, "Um-hum" and took a business card from the breast pocket of his seersucker suit. "Call me," he said, "when you've talked to the other party."

I took the card and put it in my wallet. "We're in business then," I said.

"Certainly," Macey said. "Assuming the deal is as you represent it."

"Yeah, that too," I said. "That means if we're in business that you folks will lay off old Harv here. Right?"

"Of course," Macey said. "You heard Mr. Powers. We borrow and lend, we're not animals. There's no problem there."

"Maybe not," I said. "But I want a little more reassurance. Hawk?"

Hawk was motionless on the bed, his hands folded over his solar plexus, his eyes closed. Without opening his eyes he said, "Shepard'll be okay."

I nodded. "Okay," I said. "Let's go, Harv."

Shepard put down what was left of his drink, and went out of the room without even looking around. I followed him. Nobody said goodby.

When we got in my car and started out of the parking lot, Shepard said, "How do we know they'll keep their word?"

"About staying off your back?" I said.

Shepard nodded.

"Hawk said so," I said.

"Hawk? The nigger? He's the one beat me up last time."

"He keeps his word," I said. "And I told you before, call him Hawk. I'm not going to tell you again."

"Yeah, sure, sorry, I forgot. But, Jesus, trusting him. I mean the guy Macey seems reasonable, like a guy you can do business with . . . But Hawk."

"You don't know anything," I said. "Macey would take out your eyeballs for a dollar. You think he's a guy you can deal with 'cause he talks like he went to the Wharton School. Maybe he did, but he's got no more honor than a toad. He'll do anything. Hawk won't. There's things Hawk won't do."

"Like what?"

"He won't say *yes* and do *no.*"

"Well, I guess you know your business. Where the hell are you getting the money?"

"That's not your problem," I said. We pulled up in front of Shepard's house. He'd banged back two big drinks while I was talking with Macey and his mouth was a little slow.

"Thanks, Spenser," he said. "Just for going, let alone for making that gun deal. I was scared shit."

"You should have been," I said. We shook hands, Shepard got out and went in the house. I cruised back to the motel. Susan wasn't around and her car wasn't in the lot. I called Pam Shepard from my hotel room.

"You hear from the girls?" I said.

"From Rose, yes. They'll meet us. I know you're being funny, but please don't call them girls."

"Where?"

"Where will they meet us?"

"Yeah."

"In Milton. There's an observatory on top of the Great Blue Hill. Do you know where that is?"

"Yeah."

"They'll meet us in the observatory. This afternoon at five."

I looked at my watch: 1:25. There was time. "Okay," I said. "I'll come pick you up and we'll go. I'll leave now, should be there around three. Start looking out the window then. I'll park on the street and when you see me come on down."

"What are we going to do?"

"I'll talk with you about it while we drive to Milton."

"All right."

"You bored?"

"Oh god, I'm going crazy."

"Not too much longer," I said.

"I hope not."

We hung up, I went back to my car and set out for Boston again. If I made the trip many more times I'd be able to sleep on the way. I pulled up in front of my apartment at ten after three. In about forty seconds Pam Shepard came out the front door and got in the car. And we were off again for the Blue Hills.

The top was down and Pam Shepard leaned her head back against the seat and took a big inhale. "Good god, it's good to get out of there," she said.

"That's my home you're speaking of," I said. "I was kind of wishing I could get in there."

"I didn't mean it's not nice, and it's not even so much that it's been that long, it's just that, when you know you can't go out, it's almost like claustrophobia."

Her clean brown hair was pulled back, still in the French twist she'd worn since I met her, and the wind didn't bother it much. I went out along Park Drive and the Jamaicaway and the Arborway south on Route 28. Just across the Neponset River, Route 138 branched off from Route 28 and we went with it, taking our time. We pulled into the Blue Hills Reservation and parked near the Trailside Museum at four o'clock.

"We're awfully early," Pam Shepard said.

"Plan ahead," I said. "I want to be here waiting. I don't want them to get nervous waiting for us and leave."

"I don't mind," she said. "What are we going to do?"

"We'll walk up to the observatory on the top. And when they come, I'll tell them I have a seller for them."

"A seller?"

"A gun broker. I've got a guy who'll sell them all the guns they can afford."

"But why? Why would you do that?"

"Isn't that why you stole the money?"

"Yes, but you don't approve of us, do you? You don't want to arm us certainly."

"That doesn't matter. I'm working on a very fancy move, and I don't want you trying to pretend you don't know. So I won't tell you. Then you won't have to pretend. You just assume I'm in your corner, and you vouch for me every time the question comes up."

"I've done that already. On the phone when they called. They don't trust you and they don't like you."

"Hard to imagine, isn't it," I said.

She smiled, and closed her eyes and shook her head slightly.

"Come on," I said, "let's get out and walk."

The blue hills are actually spruce green and they form the center of a large reservation of woods and ponds in an upper-middle-class suburb that abuts Boston. The biggest of the blue hills supports on its flank a nature museum, and on its crest a fieldstone observatory from which one gets a fine view of Boston's skyline, and an excellent wind for kite flying on the downside pitch of the hill below the building. It's a hike of maybe fifteen minutes to the top, through woods and over small gullies, and there are usually Cub Scout packs and Audubon members clambering among the slate-colored outcroppings. I offered Pam Shepard a hand over one of the gullies and she declined. I didn't offer on the next one. I'm a quick study.

The observatory at the top had two sets of stairs and two balconies and kids were running up and down the stairs and shouting at each other from the balconies. Several kites danced above us, one of them shaped like a large bat. "That's auspicious," I said to Pam, and nodded at the bat.

She smiled. "They have all sorts of fancy ones like that now,"

128

she said. "The kids went through the kite stage. Harvey and I could never get them to fly . . . Or us either, now that I think of it."

"It can be done," I said. "I've seen it done."

She shrugged and smiled again and shook her head. We stood on the upper balcony of the observatory and looked at the Boston skyline to the north. "What is it," Pam Shepard said, "about a cluster of skyscrapers in the distance that makes you feel . . . What? . . . Romantic? Melancholy? Excited? Excited probably."

"Promise," I said.

"Of what?"

"Of everything," I said. "From a distance they promise everything, whatever you're after. They look clean and permanent against the sky like that. Up close you notice dog litter around the foundations."

"Are you saying it's not real? The look of the skyscrapers from a distance."

"No. It's real enough, I think. But so is the dog litter and if you spend all your time looking at the spires you're going to step in it."

"Into each life some shit must fall?"

"Ah," I said, "you put it so much more gracefully than I."

She laughed.

Below us to the left Jane emerged from behind some trees where the trail opened out into a small meadow below the observatory. She looked around carefully and then looked up at us on the balcony. Pam Shepard waved. I smiled inoffensively. Jane turned her head and said something and Rose emerged from the trees and stood beside her. Pam waved again and Rose waved back. My smile became even more inoffensive. And earnest. I fairly vibrated with earnestness. This was going to be the tough part. Guys like Powers you can get with money, or the hope of it. Or fear, if you're in a position to scare them. But people like Rose, they were hard. Zealots were always hard. Zeal distorts them. Makes the normal impulses convolute. Makes people fearless and greedless and loveless and finally monstrous. I was against zeal. But being against it didn't make it go away. I had to persuade these two zealots to go along with the plan or the plan washed away and maybe so did the Shepards.

They trudged up the hill to the observatory warily, alert for an ambush among the kite-flying kids and the Cub Scouts looking at lichen growth on the north side of rocks. They disappeared below us as they went into the stairwell and then appeared coming up the stairs behind us. As Rose reached the top of the stairs Pam Shepard went to her and embraced her. Rose patted her back as they hugged. With one arm still around Rose, Pam took Jane's hand and squeezed it.

"It's good to see you both," she said.

Rose said, "Are you all right?"

Jane said, "Have you got a place to stay?"

"Yes, yes, I'm all right, I'm fine, I've been using his apartment."

"With him?" Rose looked suddenly menopausal.

"No," I said. The way I used to say it to my mother. "No, I've been down the Cape, working on a case. Besides I have a girlfriend, ah woman, ah, I have a person, I . . . I'm with Susan Silverman."

Rose said to Pam Shepard, "That's good of him."

Jane said to Rose and Pam Shepard, "I still don't trust him."

"You can," Pam said. "You really can. I trust him. He's a good man."

I smiled harder. Ingratiation. Jane eyed me for vulnerable points.

Rose said, "Well, whether or not we can trust him, we can talk some business with him at least. I'll reserve my opinion of his trustworthiness. What is his offer exactly?" And, while she hadn't yet addressed me directly, she looked at me. Once they did that I always had them. I think it was the puckish charm. "Well?" she said. Yeah, it was the puckish charm.

"I can get you all the guns you need, one hundred thousand dollars' worth. And bullets. No questions asked."

"Why?"

"I get a broker's fee."

Rose nodded. Jane said, "Perhaps that's why we can trust him."

Rose said, "I suppose we give you the money and then you have the guns delivered? Something like that perhaps? And when we get tired of waiting for delivery and call you up you seem to have moved?"

Pam Shepard said, "No. Rose, believe me, you can trust him. He's not dishonest."

"Pam, almost everyone is dishonest. He's as dishonest as anyone else. I don't want to do business with him."

"That's dumb," I said. "It's the kind of dumb that smart people get because they think they're smart."

"What the hell does that mean?" Jane said.

"It means that if everyone's dishonest you aren't going to do better elsewhere. And the devil you know is better than the devil you don't know. I got one character witness. Where you going to find a gun dealer that has that many?"

Rose said, "We are not fools. You assume women can't manage this sort of thing? That gunrunning is a masculine profession?"

"I don't assume anything. What I know is that amateurs can't handle this sort of thing. You will get ripped off if you're lucky and ripped off and busted if you're not." Ah, Spenser, master of the revolutionary argot. Word haven of the counterculture.

"And why should we believe you won't rip us off?" Jane said.

"You got my word, and the assurance of one of your own people. Have I lied to you yet? Have I turned Pam in to her husband, or the fuzz? You held up a bank and killed an old man. He used to be a cop and the New Bedford cops are not going to forget that. They are going to be looking for you until Harvard wins the Rose Bowl. You are fugitives from justice as the saying goes. And you are in no position to be advertising for a gun dealer. If the word gets out that a group of women are looking to make a gun buy, who do you think the first dealer will be? The easy one, the one that shows up one day and says he's got what you want?"

"So far," Rose said, "it seems to be you."

"Yeah, and you know who I am. The next one will be somebody undercover. An FBI informant, a special services cop, an agent from the Treasury Department, maybe a woman, a nice black woman with all the proper hatreds who wants to help out a sister. And you show up with the cash and she shows up with thirteen cops and the paddy wagon."

"He's right, you know," Pam Shepard said. "He knows about this kind of thing, and we don't. Who would get us guns that we could trust better?"

"Perhaps," Rose said, "we can merely sit on the money for a while."

I shook my head. "No, you can't. Then you're just a felon, a robber and murderer. Now you're a revolutionary who killed because she had to. If you don't do what you set out to do then you have no justification for murdering that old man and the guilt will get you."

"I killed the guard," Jane said. "Rose didn't. He tried to stop us and I shot him." She seemed proud.

"Same, same," I said. "She's an accessory and as responsible as you are. Doesn't matter who squeezed off the round."

"We can do without the amateur psychoanalyzing, Spenser," Rose said. "How do we prevent you from taking our money and running?"

"I'll just be the broker. You and the gun dealer meet face to face. You see the guns, he sees the money."

"And if they're defective?"

"Examine them before you buy."

They were silent.

"If you're not familiar with the particular type of weapon, I'll examine it too. Have you thought of what kinds of guns you want?"

"Any kind," Jane said. "Just so they fire."

"No, Jane. Let's be honest. We don't know much about guns. You know that anyway. We want guns appropriate for guerrilla fighting. Including handguns that we can conceal easily, and, I should think, some kind of machine guns."

"You mean hand-held automatic weapons, you don't mean something you'd mount on a tripod."

"That's right. Whatever the proper terminology. Does that seem sensible to you?"

"Yeah. Let me check with my dealer. Any other preferences?"

"Just so they shoot," Jane said.

"Are we in business?" I said.

"Let us talk a bit, Mr. Spenser," Rose said. And the three women walked to the other end of the balcony and huddled.

On the walls of the observatory, mostly in spray paint, were graffiti. Mostly names, but also a pitch for gay liberation, a suggestion that blacks be bused to Africa and some remarks about the sister of somebody named Mangan. The conference broke up and Rose came back and said, "All right, we're agreed. When can you get the guns?"

"I'll have to be in touch with you," I said. "Couple days, probably."

"We're not giving you an address or phone number."

"No need to." I gave her my card. "You have my number. I'll leave a message with my answering service. Call every day at noon and check in. Collect is okay."

"We'll pay our way, Mr. Spenser."

"Of course you will, I was just being pleasant."

"Perhaps you shouldn't bother, Mr. Spenser. It seems very hard for you."

22

ROSE AND JANE left as furtively as they'd come. They were hooked. I might pull it off. Jane hadn't even kicked me.

"It's going to work," I said to Pam Shepard.

"Are they going to get hurt?"

"That's my worry, not yours."

"But I'm like the Judas goat if they are. They are trusting you because of me."

We were driving back into Boston passing the outbound commuting traffic. "Somebody has to go down," I said, "for the bank guard. It isn't going to be you and that's all you have to concentrate on."

"Damnit, Spenser, am I selling them out?"

"Yes," I said.

"You son of a bitch."

"If you kick me in the groin while I'm driving a traffic accident might ensue."

"I won't do it. I'll warn them now. As soon as I get home."

"First, you don't know how to reach them except through an ad in the paper, which you can't do right now. Second, if you warn them you will screw yourself and your husband, whose troubles are as serious as yours and whose salvation is tied to selling out Rose and Jane."

"What's wrong? What's the matter with Harvey? Are the kids okay?"

"Everyone's okay at the moment. But Harv's in hock to a loan shark. I didn't want to tell you all this but you can't trust me if I lie to you. You kept asking."

"You have no right to manipulate me. Not even for my own good. You have not got that right maybe especially for my own good."

"I know. That's why I'm telling you. You're better off not knowing, but you have the right to know and I don't have the right to decide for you."

"So what in hell is going on?"

I told her. By the time I got through we were heading down Boylston Street through Copley Square with the sun reflecting off the empty John Hancock Building and the fountain sparkling in the plaza. I left out only the part about Hawk shoving one of the kids. Paternalism is hard to shake.

"Good Jesus," she said. "What the hell have we become."

"You've become endangered species among other things. The only way out for you is to do what I say. That includes throwing Rose and Jane off the back of the sleigh."

"I can't . . . double-cross them. I know that sounds melodramatic but I don't know how else to put it."

"It's better than saying you can't betray them. But however you put it, you're wrong. You've gotten yourself into a place where all the choices are lousy. But they seem clear. You've got kids that need a mother, you've got a husband that needs a wife. You've got a life and it needs you to live it. You're a handsome intelligent broad in the middle of something that could still be a good life." I turned left at Bonwit's onto Berkeley Street. "Somebody has got to go inside for that old cop. And I won't be crying if it's Rose and Jane. They snuffed him like a candle when he got in their way. And if we can hook King Powers on the same line, I say we've done good."

I turned right onto Marlborough Street and pulled into the curb by the hydrant in front of my apartment. We went up in silence. And we were silent when we got inside. The silence got awkward inside because it was pregnant with self-awareness. We were awkwardly aware that we were alone together in my apartment and that awareness hung between us as if Kate Millett had never been born. "I'll make us some supper," I said. "Want a drink first?" My voice was a little husky but I didn't want to clear my throat. That would have been embarrassing, like an old Leon Errol movie.

"Are you having one?" she said.

"I'm having a beer." My voice had gone from husky to hoarse. I coughed to conceal the fact that I was clearing it.

"I'll have one too," she said.

I got two cans of Utica Club cream ale out of the refrigerator.

"Glass?" I said.

"No, can's fine," she said.

"Ever try this," I said. "Really very good. Since they stopped importing Amstel, I've been experimenting around."

"It's very nice," she said.

"Want spaghetti?"

"Sure, that would be fine."

I took a container of sauce from the freezer and ran it under hot water and popped the crimson block of frozen sauce out into a saucepan. I put the gas on very low under the pan, covered it and drank some Utica Club cream ale.

"When I was a kid, I remember being out in western Mass some and they used to advertise Utica Club with a little character made out of the U and the C. I think he was called Ukie." I coughed again, and finished the beer. Pam Shepard was leaning her backside on one of the two counter stools in my kitchen, her legs straight out in front of her and slightly apart so that the light summer print dress she wore pulled tight over the tops of her thighs. I wondered if tumescent could be a noun. I am a tumescent? Sounded good. She sipped a little of the beer from the can.

"Like it?" I said.

She nodded.

"And the plan? How about that."

She shook her head.

"All right, you don't like it. But will you go along? Don't waste yourself. Go along. I can get you out of this mess. Let me."

"Yes," she said. "I'm not pleased with myself, but I'll go along. For Harvey and for the children and for myself. Probably mostly for myself . . ."

Ah-ha, the old puckish charm. I must use this power only for good.

I said, "Whew" and popped the top off another can of Utica Club. I put the water on for the spaghetti and started to tear lettuce for the salad.

"Want another beer," I said. I put the lettuce in some ice water to crisp.

"Not yet," she said. She sat still and sipped on the beer and watched me. I glanced at her occasionally and smiled and tried not to look too long at her thighs.

"I can't figure you out," she said.

I sliced a red onion paper thin with a wide-bladed butcher knife.

"You mean how someone with my looks and talent ended up in this kind of business?"

"I was thinking more about all the conflicts in your character. You reek of machismo, and yet you are a very caring person. You have all these muscles and yet you read all those books. You're sarcastic and a wise guy and you make fun of everything; and yet you were really afraid I'd say no a little while ago and two people you don't even like all that well would get into trouble. And now here you are cooking me my supper and you're obviously nervous at being alone with me in your apartment."

"Obviously?"

"Obviously."

"And you?"

"I too. But I'm just somebody's middle-class housewife. I would have assumed that you were used to such things. Surely I can't be the first woman you've made supper for?"

"I cook for Suze a lot," I said. I cut some native tomatoes into wedges. And started on a green pepper.

"And for no one else?"

"Lately, just for Suze."

"So what's different about me? Why is there this sense of strain?"

"I'm not sure. It has to do with you being desirable and me being randy. I know that much. But it also has to do with a sense that we should leave it at that."

"Why?" She had put the beer can down and her arms were folded under her breasts.

"I'm trying to get you and Harv back together and making a move at you doesn't seem the best way to get that done. And, I don't think Suze would like it all that much either."

"Why would she have to know?"

"Because if I didn't tell her then there would be things I kept from her. She couldn't trust me."

"But she wouldn't know she couldn't trust you."

"Yeah, but she couldn't."

"That's crazy."

"No. See the fact would be that she couldn't trust me. That I am not trustworthy. The fact that she didn't know it would be simply another deception."

"So you confess every indiscretion?"

"Every one she has a right to know about."

"Have there been many?"

"Some."

"And Susan objects?"

"No. Not generally. But she doesn't know them. And she knows you. I think this would hurt her. Especially now. We're at some kind of juncture. I'm not quite sure what, but I think this would be wrong. Damnit."

"She is, I think, a very lucky woman."

"Would you be willing to swear to that. Just recently she called me a horse's ass."

"That's possible," Pam Shepard said.

I sliced up three small pickling cucumbers, skin and all, and added them to my salad. I took the lettuce out of the water and patted it with a towel and then wrapped it and put it in the refrigerator. I checked my sauce, it was nearly melted. I added some seedless green grapes to the salad bowl. "The thing is, all that explanation didn't do much for the randiness. I don't think it's fatal, but you can't say I'm resting comfortably."

Pam Shepard laughed. "That's good to know. In fact, I thought about us going to bed together and the thought was pleasant. You look like you'd hurt and somehow I know you wouldn't."

"Tough but oh so gentle," I said.

"But it isn't going to happen, and it's probably just as well. I don't usually feel so good about myself after I've made it with someone but Harvey." She laughed again, but this time harshly. "Come to think about it, I didn't feel all that good the last few times I made it with Harvey."

"Was that recently?"

She looked away from me. "Two years ago."

"That embarrass you?"

She looked back. "Yes," she said. "Very much. Don't you think it should?"

"Yeah, maybe. On the other hand you're not a sex vend-omatic. He drops in two quarters and you come across. I guess you didn't want to sleep with him."

"I couldn't stand it."

"And you both figured you were frigid. So you hustled out evenings to prove you weren't."

"I guess so. Not very pretty, is it?"

"Nope. Unhappiness never is. How about Harv, what was he doing to dissipate tension?"

"Dissipate tension. My god, I don't think I've ever heard anyone talk the way you do. I don't know what he was doing. Masturbation perhaps. I don't think he was with other women."

"Why not?"

"Loyalty, masochism, maybe love, who knows."

"Maybe a way to grind the guilt in deeper too."

"Maybe, maybe all that."

"It's almost always all that. It seems the longer I'm in business, the more it's always everything working at the same time." I took two cans of Utica Club from the refrigerator and popped the tops and handed one to her.

"The thing is," she said, "I never found out."

"If you were frigid?"

"Yes. I'd get drunk and I'd thrash around and bite and moan and do anything anyone wanted done, but part of it all was faking and the next day I was always disgusted. I think one reason I wanted to ball you was so I could ask you afterwards if you thought I was frigid." Her voice had a harsh sound to it, and when she said "ball you" it sounded wrong in her mouth. I knew the harsh sound. Disgust, I'd heard it before.

"For one thing, you're asking the wrong question. Frigid isn't a very useful word. You pointed that out to me a while ago. It doesn't have a meaning. It simply means you don't want to do something that someone else wants you to do. If you don't enjoy screwing old Harv then why not say that. Why generalize. Say I don't enjoy screwing Harvey, or, even better, I didn't enjoy it last evening. Why turn it into an immutable law."

"It's not that simple."

"Sometimes I wonder. Sometimes I think everything is that simple. But you're probably right. Sex is as natural as breathing except it takes a partner and what one can do with ease, two mangle."

"Does Susan . . . I'm sorry, I have no right to ask that."

"Does Susan like to have sexual intercourse? Sometimes she does and sometimes she doesn't. Occasionally, just occasionally now, that's true of me. The occasions are more frequent than they were when I was nineteen."

She smiled.

I took the lettuce out of the refrigerator, unwrapped it and tossed it in the bowl with the rest of the vegetables. My sauce was starting to bubble gently and I took enough spaghetti for two and tossed it into my boiling kettle. "Plenty of water," I said, "makes it less sticky, and it comes right back to a boil so it starts cooking right away. See that. I am a spaghetti superstar."

"Why do you want Harvey and me back together? I'm not sure that's your business. Or is it just America and apple pie. Marriages are made in heaven, they should never break up?"

"I just don't think you've given it a real shot."

"A real shot. Twenty-two years? That's not a real shot?"

"That's a long shot, but not a real one. You've been trying to be what you aren't until you can't swallow it anymore and now you think you're frigid. He's been panting after greatness all his life and he can't catch it because he thinks it's success."

"If I'm not what I've been trying to be, what am I?"

"I don't know. Maybe you could find out if you no longer decided that what you ought to be was what your husband expected you to be."

"I'm not sure I know what you're talking about."

"You too, huh? Well, look, if he's disappointed in you it

doesn't mean you're wrong. It could mean he's wrong."

She shook her head. "Of course, I mean that's no news flash. That's every woman's problem. I know that."

"Don't generalize on me. I don't know if it's every woman's problem, or if it's only a woman's problem. What I do know is that it might be one of your problems. If so, it can be solved. It's one thing to know something. It's another to feel it, to act as if it were so, in short, to believe it."

"And how does one learn to believe something?"

"One talks for a while with a good psychotherapist."

"Oh god, a shrink?"

"There's good ones and bad ones. Like private eyes. I can put you in touch with some good ones."

"Former clients?"

"No, Suze knows a lot about that stuff. She's a guidance person and takes it seriously."

"Is that the answer, a damned shrink? Everything that happens some psychiatrist is in on it. Every time some kid gets an F the shrink's got to have his two cents' worth."

"You ever try it?"

"No."

"Harv?"

"No. He wanted me to, see if they could find out why I was frigid. But he didn't want to go too. Said there was nothing wrong with him. Didn't want some goddamned headshrinker prying around in his business trying to convince him he was sick."

"Doesn't have to be a psychiatrist, you know. Could be a good social worker. You ought to talk with Suze about it. But Harv's got the wrong language again, just like frigid. Doesn't help to talk about 'wrong' with a big W. You got a problem. They can help. Sometimes."

"What about all these people they commit to asylums for no reason and how in murder cases they can't agree on anything. One side gets a shrink to say he's crazy and the other side gets one to say he's sane."

"Okay, psychiatry boasts as many turkeys as any other business, maybe more. But the kinds of things you're talking about aren't relevant. Those things come from asking psychiatrists to do what they aren't equipped to do. Good ones know that, I think. Good ones know that what they can do is help people work out problems. I don't think they are very good at curing schizophrenia or deciding whether someone is legally sane. That's bullshit. But they might be quite useful in helping you get over defining yourself in your husband's terms, or helping your husband get over defining himself in Cotton Mather's terms."

"Cotton Mather?"

"Yeah, you know, the old Puritan ethic."

"Oh, that Cotton Mather. You do read the books, don't you?"

"I got a lotta time," I said. The timer buzzed and I twirled out a strand of spaghetti and tried it. "Al dente," I said. "His brother Sam used to play for the Red Sox." The spaghetti was done, I turned it into a colander, emptied the pan, shook the colander to drain the spaghetti, turned it back into the pan, added a little butter and some Parmesan cheese and tossed it.

"You made that up."

"What?"

"About Al Dente's brother."

"Nope. Truth. Sam Dente used to play with the Sox about thirty years ago. Infielder. Left-handed batter." The spaghetti sauce was bubbling. I poured it into a big gravy boat and put two big heaps of spaghetti on two plates. I poured the salad dressing over the salad, tossed it and set everything on the kitchen counter. "Silverware in the drawer there," I said. I got some Gallo Burgundy in a half-gallon bottle and two wine glasses out of the cupboard.

We sat at the counter and ate and drank. "Did you make the spaghetti sauce?" she said.

"Yeah. A secret recipe I got off the back of the tomato paste can."

"And the salad dressing? Is there honey in it?"

"Yep. Got that from my mother."

She shook her head. "Fighter, lover, gourmet cook? Amazing."

"Nope. I'll take the fighter, lover, but the gourmet cook is a sexist remark."

"Why?"

"If you'd cooked this no one would say you were a gourmet cook. It's because I'm a man. A man who cooks and is interested in it is called a gourmet. A woman is called a housewife. Now eat the goddamned spaghetti," I said. She did. Me too.

23

I SLEPT on the couch. A triumph once more of virtue over tumescence. I was up and showered and away before Pam Shepard woke up. At 10:00 A.M. I was having coffee with King Powers' man Macey in the Holiday Inn in Hyannis.

"Care for some fruit?" Macey said.

"No thanks. The coffee will do. When can you deliver the guns?"

"Tomorrow maybe, day after for sure."

"What you got?"

"M2 carbines, in perfect condition, one hundred rounds apiece."

"How many?"

"Four hundred and fifty."

"Jesus Christ, that's more than two bills apiece."

Macey shrugged. "Ammo's included, don't forget."

"Christ, you can pick 'em up in the gun shop for less than half that."

"Four hundred and fifty of them? M2s?"

"There's that," I said. "But a hundred grand for four hundred and fifty pieces. I don't think my people will like that."

"You came to us, Spence. You asked us. Remember."

I loved being called Spence. "And remember there's thirty thousand out for your share."

"Which you're keeping."

"Hey, Spence, it's owed us. We wouldn't be long in business if we didn't demand financial responsibility from our clients. We didn't go to Harvey either. He came to us. Just like you. You don't like the deal, you're free to make another one someplace else. Just see to it that Harvey comes up with the thirty thousand dollars he owes us. Which, incidentally, will increase as of Monday."

"Oh yeah, you private-service firms seem to work on an escalated interest scale, don't you."

Macey smiled and shrugged and spread his hands. "What can I tell you, Spence? We have our methods and we attract clients. We must be doing something right." He folded his arms. "You want the guns or don't you?"

"Yes."

"Good, then we have a deal. When do you wish to take delivery? I can guarantee day after tomorrow." He checked his calendar watch. "The twenty-seventh. Sooner is iffy."

"The twenty-seventh is fine."

"And where do you wish to take delivery?"

"Doesn't matter. You got a spot?"

"Yes. Do you know the market terminal in Chelsea?"

"Yeah."

"There, day after tomorrow at six A.M. There are a lot of trucks loading and unloading at that time. No one will pay us any mind. Your principals have a truck?"

"Yeah."

"Okay. We've got a deal. You going to be there with your people?"

"Yeah."

"I won't be. But you should have ready for the man in charge one hundred thousand dollars in cash. Go to the restaurant there in the market center. You know where it is." I nodded. "Have a cup of coffee or whatever. You'll be contacted."

"No good," I said.

"Why not?"

"King's got to deliver them himself."

"Why?"

"My people want to do business with the principals. They don't like working through me. They might want to do more business and they want to deal direct."

"Perhaps I can go."

"No. It's gotta be King. They want to be sure they don't get burned. They figure doing business with the boss is like earnest money. If he does it himself they figure it'll go right, there won't be anything sour, like selling us ten crates of lead pipe. Or shooting us and taking the money and going away. They figure King wouldn't want to be involved in that kind of goings-on himself. Too much risk. So, King delivers personally or it's no deal."

"Mr. Powers doesn't like being told what to do," Macey said.

"Me either, but we been reasonable, and you're getting your price. He can bend on this one."

"I can assure you there will be no contrivances or double-dealing on this. This is an on-the-table, straight-ahead business deal."

"That's good to know, Macey. And I believe you 'cause I'm here looking into your sincere brown eyes but my clients, they're not here. They don't know how sincere you are and they don't trust you. Even after I mentioned how you been to college and everything."

"How about we just cancel the whole thing and foreclose on Harvey."

"We go to the cops."

"And Harvey explains why he needed all that money we advanced him?"

"Better than explaining to you people why he can't pay."

"That would be a bad mistake."

"Yeah, maybe, but it would be a bad one for you too. Even if you wasted Harvey you'd have the fuzzy-wuzzies following you around and you'd have me mad at you and trying to get you busted and for what? All because King was too lazy to get up one morning for a six o'clock appointment?"

Macey looked at me for maybe thirty seconds.

"You don't want to maneuver me and Harv into a place where we got no options. You don't want to make the law look more attractive than you guys. You don't want to arrange something where Harv's got nothing to lose by talking to the D.A. My people are adamant on this. They are interested in doing business with the man. And you ain't him. King is the man."

Macey said, "I'll check with him. I'm not authorized to commit him to something like this."

"You're not authorized to zip your fly without asking King. We both know that, preppy. Call him." Macey looked at me another thirty seconds. Then he got up and went into the next room.

He was gone maybe fifteen minutes. I drank my coffee and admired my Adidas Varsities, in rust-colored suede. Excellent for tennis, jogging and avoiding injury through flight. I poured another cup of coffee from the room service thermos pitcher. It was not hot. I left the cup on the table and went to the window and looked down at the pool. It was as blue as heaven and full of people, largely young ones, splashing and swimming and diving. A lot of flesh was darkening on beach chairs around the pool and some of it was pleasant to see. I should probably call Susan. I hadn't been back last night. Maybe she'd be worried. I should have called her last night. Hard to keep everything in my head sometimes. Pam Shepard and Harvey and Rose and Jane and King Powers and Hawk, and the New Bedford cops and getting it to work. And the tumescence. There was that to deal with too. A girl with long straight blond hair appeared from under one of the sun umbrellas wearing a bikini so brief as to seem pointless. I was looking at her closely when Macey came back into the room.

"King okayed it."

"Say, isn't that good," I said. "Not only is he a King but he's a Prince. Right, Macey?"

"He wasn't easy to persuade, Spence. You've got me to thank for this deal. He was going to have you blown away when I first told him what you wanted."

"And you saved me. Macey, you've put it all together today, kid."

"You laugh, but I'm telling you it was a near thing. This better go smooth or King'll do it. Take my word. He'll do it, Spence."

"Macey," I said. "If you call me Spence again I'll break your glasses."

24

IT WAS ELEVEN-TWENTY when I got back to my motel. There was a note on the bureau. "I'm walking on the beach," it said. "Be back around lunchtime. Maybe I didn't come home all night either." I looked at my watch: 11:20. I called my service and left word for Rose to call me at the motel. At five past twelve she did.

"You know where the New England Produce Center is in Chelsea?" I said.

"No."

"I'm going to tell you, so get a pencil and write it down."

"I have one."

I told her. "When you get there," I said, "go to the restaurant and sit at the counter and have a cup of coffee. I'll be there by quarter of six."

"I want Pamela to be there as well."

"Why?"

"I'll trust you more if she's there."

"That's sort of like using a sister," I said.

"We use what we must. The cause requires it."

"Always does," I said.

"She'll be there?"

"I'll bring her with me."

"We will be there, with our part of the bargain."

"You'll need a truck."

"How large?"

"Not large, an Econoline van, something like that."

"We'll rent one. Will you help us load?"

"Yes."

"Very well. See you there." She hung up.

I wrote a note to Susan, told her I'd be back to take her to dinner, put twenty-seven X's at the bottom and replaced the one she'd written me. Then I called New Bedford. Jackie Sylvia said he and McDermott would meet me at the Bristol County Court House on County Street. They were there when I arrived, leaning on each side of a white pillar out front.

"Come on," Sylvia said when I got out of the car. "We got to talk with Linhares."

We went into the red brick courthouse, past the clerk's office, up some stairs and into an office that said ANTON LINHARES, ASST. DIST. ATT., on the door. Linhares stood, came around the desk and shook hands with me when we went in. He was medium-size and trim with a neat Afro haircut, a dark three-piece suit and a white shirt with a black and red regimental stripe tie. His shoes looked like Gucci and his suit looked like Pierre Cardin and he looked like a future D.A. His handshake was firm and he smelled of after shave lotion. Canoe I bet.

"Sit down, Spenser, good to see you. Jackie and Rich have me wired in on the case. I don't see any problem. When's it going down?"

"Day after tomorrow," I said, "at six in the morning, at the market terminal in Chelsea."

"That Suffolk or Middlesex County?"

"Suffolk," I said.

"You sure?"

"I used to work for the Suffolk County D.A. Everett's Middlesex, Chelsea's Suffolk."

"Okay, I'm going to need some cooperation from Suffolk." He looked at his wristwatch. It was big and had a luminous green face and you pressed a button to get the time displayed in digits. "That's no sweat," he said. "I'll get Jim Clancy on the horn up there. He'll go along."

He leaned back in his swivel chair, cocked one foot up on a slightly open drawer and looked at me. "What's the setup?" he said. I told him.

"So we set up around there ahead of time," Sylvia said, "and when they are in the middle of the transaction . . ." He raised an open hand and clamped it shut.

Linhares nodded. "Right. We've got them no matter what part of the swap they're in. One of them will have stolen money and the others will have stolen guns. I want to be there. I want part of this one."

McDermott said, "We thought you might, Anton."

Linhares smiled without irritation. "I didn't take this job to stay in it all my life."

Sylvia said, "Yeah, but let's make sure this doesn't get leaked to the press before it happens."

Linhares grinned again. "Gentlemen," he said. He shook his head in friendly despair. "Gentlemen. How unkind."

"Sylvia's right," I said. "These are very careful people. King Powers by habit. Rose and Jane by temperament. They'll be very skittish."

"Fair enough," Linhares said. "Now what about your people. How you want to handle that?"

"I want them not to exist," I said. "They can be referred to as two anonymous undercover operatives whose identity must be protected. Me too. If my name gets into this it may drag theirs in with it. They're both clients."

Linhares said, "I'll need the names. Not to prosecute but to bury. If they get scooped up in the net I've got to know who to let go."

I told him. "They're related?" he said.

"Yeah, husband and wife."

"And you put this thing together for them?"

"Yeah."

"How'd Suffolk ever let you get away?"

"Hard to figure," I said.

"Okay." Linhares looked at his watch again. He liked pushing the button. "Jackie, you and Rich get up there tomorrow with Spenser here and set this thing up. I'll call Jimmy Clancy and have him waiting for you."

"We gotta check with the squad," McDermott said.

"I'll take care of that," Linhares said. "I'll call Sergeant Cruz and have you assigned to me for a couple days. Manny and I are buddies. He'll go along. You get hold of Bobby Santos, he'll go up with you tomorrow so he can brief me for the bust." He reached over and punched an intercom on his phone and said into it, "Peggy, get me Jimmy Clancy up in the Suffolk D.A.'s office." With one hand over the mouthpiece he said to me, "Good seeing you, Spenser. Nice job on this one." And to Sylvia and McDermott, "You, too, guys, nice job all around."

He took his hand away and said into the phone, "Jimmy, Anton Linhares. I got a live one for you, kid." We got up and went out.

"Who's this Santos?" I said to Jackie Sylvia.

"State dick, works out of this office. He's okay. Wants to be public safety commissioner, but what the hell, nothing wrong with ambition. Right, Rich?"

"I don't know," McDermott said. "I never had any. You want to ride up with us tomorrow, Spenser, or you want to meet us there?"

"I'll meet you there," I said. "In Clancy's office. About ten."

"Catch you then," Sylvia said. We reached my car. There was a parking ticket under the windshield wiper. I took it out and slipped it into the breast pocket of Sylvia's maroon blazer. "Show me the kind of clout you got around here," I said. "Fix that." I got in the car. As I pulled away Sylvia took the ticket out of his pocket and tore it in two. As I pulled around the corner on County Street he was giving half to McDermott.

I was into the maze again and on my first pass at the Fairhaven Bridge I ended up going out Acushnet Street parallel to the river. There was a parking lot by the unemployment office and I pulled in to turn around. There was a long line at the unemployment office and a man with a pushcart and a striped umbrella was selling hot dogs, soft drinks, popcorn and peanuts. Festive.

I made the bridge on my second try, and headed back down the Cape. The sun was at my back now and ahead was maybe a swim, some tennis and supper. I hoped Susan hadn't eaten. It was five-twenty when I got back to the motel. I spotted Susan's Nova in the lot. When I unlocked the door to the room she was there. Sitting in front of the mirror with a piece of Kleenex in her hand, her hair up in big rollers, a lot of cream on her face, wearing a flowered robe and unlaced sneakers.

"Arrrgh," I said.

"You weren't supposed to be back yet," she said, wiping at some of the cream with her Kleenex.

"Never mind that shit, lady," I said, "what have you done with Susan Silverman?"

"It's time you knew, sweetie, this is the real me."

"Heavens," I said.

"Does this mean it's over?"

"No, but tell me the fake you will reappear in a while."

"Twenty minutes," she said. "I've made us reservations at the Coonamessett Inn for seven."

"How about a swim first and then some tennis, or vice versa."

"No. I just washed my hair. I don't want to get it wet and sweaty. Or vice versa. Why don't you swim while I conceal the real me. Then we can have a drink and a leisurely drive to the inn and you can explain yourself and where the hell you've been and what you've been doing and with or to whom, and that sort of thing."

I swam for a half-hour. The pool was only about fifty feet long so I did a lot of turns, but it was a nice little workout and I went back to the room with the blood moving in my veins. Susan didn't do anything to slow it down. The hair was unrolled and the robe and cream had disappeared. And she was wearing a pale sleeveless dress the color of an eggshell, and jade earrings. She was putting her lipstick on when I came in, leaning close to the mirror to make sure it was right.

I took a shower and shaved and brushed my teeth with a fluoride toothpaste that tasted like Christmas candy. I put on my dark blue summer suit with brass buttons on the coat and vest, a pale blue oxford button-down shirt and a white tie with blue and gold stripes. Dark socks, black tassel loafers. I checked myself in the mirror. Clear-eyed, and splendid. I clipped my gun on under my coat. I really ought to get a dress gun sometime. A pearl handle perhaps, in a patent leather holster.

"Stay close to me," I said to Susan on the way out to the car. "The Hyannis Women's Club may try to kidnap me and treat me as a sex object."

Susan put her arm through mine. "Death before dishonor," she said.

In the car Susan put a kerchief over her hair and I drove

slowly with the top down to the inn. We had a Margarita in the bar and a table by the window where you could look out on the lake.

We had a second Margarita while we looked at the menu. "No beer?" Susan asked.

"Didn't seem to go with the mood or the occasion," I said. "I'll have some with dinner."

I ordered raw oysters and lobster thermidor. Susan chose oysters and baked stuffed lobster.

"It's all falling into place, Suze," I said. "I think I can do it."

"I hope so," she said. "Have you seen Pam Shepard?"

"Last night."

"Oh?"

"Yeah, I slept in my apartment last night."

"Oh? How is she?"

"Oh, nowhere near as good as you," I said.

"I don't mean that. I mean how is her state of mind."

"Okay, I think you should talk with her. She's screwed up pretty good, and I think she needs some kind of therapy."

"Why? You made a pass at her and she turned you down?"

"Just talk with her. I figure you can direct her someplace good. She and her husband can't agree on what she ought to be and she feels a lot of guilt about that."

Susan nodded. "Of course I'll talk with her. When?"

"After this is over, day after tomorrow it should be."

"I'll be glad to."

"I didn't make a pass at her."

"I didn't ask," Susan said.

"It was a funny scene though. I mean we talked about it a lot. She's not a fool, but she's misled, maybe unadult, it's hard to put my finger on it. She believes some very destructive things. What's that Frost line, 'He will not go behind his father's saying'?"

"'Mending Wall,'" Susan said.

"Yeah, she's like that, like she never went beyond her mother's sayings, or her father's and when they didn't work she still didn't go beyond them. She just found someone with a new set of sayings, and never went beyond them."

"Rose and Jane?" Susan said.

"You have a fine memory," I said. "It helps make up for your real appearance."

"There's a lot of women like that. I see a lot of them at school, and a lot of them at school parties. Wives of teachers and principals. I see a lot of them coming in with their daughters and I see a lot of daughters that will grow into that kind of woman."

"Frost was writing about a guy," I said.

"Yes, I know. I see." The waitress brought our oysters. "It's not just women, is it."

"No, ma'am. Old Harv is just as bad, just as far into the sayings of his father and just as blind to what's beyond them as Pam is."

"Doesn't he need therapy too?"

The oysters were outstanding. Very fresh, very young. "Yeah, I imagine. But I think she might be brighter, and have more guts. I don't think he's got the guts for therapy. Maybe not the brains either. But I've only seen him under stress. Maybe he's better than he looks," I said. "He loves her. Loves the crap out of her."

"Maybe that's just another saying of his father's that he can't go behind."

"Maybe everything's a saying. Maybe there isn't anything but saying. You have to believe in something. Loving the crap out of someone isn't the worst one."

"Ah, you sweet talker you," Susan said. "How elegantly you put it. Do you love the crap out of anyone?"

"You got it, sweetheart," I said.

"Is that your Bogart impression again?"

"Yeah, I work on it in the car mirror driving back and forth between here and Boston and New Bedford."

The oysters departed and the lobster came. While we worked on it I told Susan everything we had set up for the next day. Few people can match Susan Silverman for lobster eating. She leaves no claw uncracked, no crevice unpried. And all the while she doesn't get any on her and she doesn't look savage.

I tend to hurt myself when I attack a baked stuffed lobster. So I normally get thermidor, or salad, or stew or whatever they offered that had been shelled for me.

When I got through talking Susan said, "It's hard to keep it all in your head, isn't it. So many things depend on so many other things. So much is unresolved and will remain so unless every-thing goes in sequence."

"Yeah, it's nervous-making."

"You don't seem nervous."

"It's what I do," I said. "I'm good at it. It'll probably work."

"And if it doesn't."

"Then it's a mess and I'll have to think of something else. But I've done what I can. I try not to worry about things I can't control."

"And you assume if it breaks you can fix it, don't you?"

"I guess so. Something like that. I've always been able to do most of what I needed to do."

We each had a very good wild blueberry tart for dessert and retired to the bar for Irish coffee. On the ride back to the motel, Susan put her head back against the seat without the kerchief and let her hair blow about.

"Want to go look at the ocean," I said.

"Yes," she said.

I drove down Sea Street to the beach and parked in the lot. It was late and there was no one there. Susan left her shoes in the car and we walked along the sand in the bright darkness with the ocean rolling in gently to our left. I took her hand and we walked in silence. Off somewhere to the right, inland, someone was playing an old Tommy Dorsey album and a vocal group was singing "Once in a While." The sound in the late stillness drifted out across the water. Quaint and sort of old-fashioned now, and familiar.

"Want to swim," I said.

We dropped our clothes in a heap on the beach and went into the ebony water and swam beside each other parallel to the shore perhaps a quarter of a mile. Susan was a strong swimmer and I didn't have to slow down for her. I dropped back slightly so I could watch the white movement of her arms and shoulders as they sliced almost soundlessly through the water. We could still hear the stereo. A boy singer was doing "East of the Sun and West of the Moon" with a male vocal group for backing. Ahead of me Susan stopped and stood breast deep in the water. I stopped beside her and put my arms around her slick body. She was breathing deeply, though not badly out of breath, and I could feel her heart beating strongly against my chest. She kissed me and the salt taste of ocean mixed with the sweet taste of her lipstick. She pulled her head back and looked up at me with her hair plastered tight against her scalp. And the beads of sea water glistening on her face. Her teeth seemed very shiny to me, up close like that when she smiled.

"In the water?" she said.

"Never tried it in the water," I said. My voice was hoarse again.

"I'll drown," she said and turned and dove toward the shore. I plunged after her and caught her at the tidal margin and we lay in the wet sand and made love while Frank Sinatra and the Pied Pipers sang "There Are Such Things" and the waves washed about our legs. By the time we had finished the late-night listener had put on an Artie Shaw album and we were listening to "Dancing in the Dark." We were motionless for a bit, letting the waves flow over us. The tide seemed to be coming in. A wave larger than the ones before it broke over us, and for a moment we were underwater. We came up, both of us blowing water from our mouths, and looked at each other and began to laugh. "Deborah Kerr," I said.

"Burt Lancaster," she said.

"From here to eternity," I said.

"That far, at least," she said. And we snuggled in the wet sand with the sea breaking over us until our teeth began to chatter.

25

WE GOT DRESSED and went back to the motel and took a long hot shower together and ordered a bottle of Burgundy from room service and got into bed and sipped the wine and watched the late movie, *Fort Apache,* one of my favorites, and fell asleep.

In the morning we had breakfast in the room and when I left for Boston about eight-thirty, Susan was still in bed, drinking a cup of coffee and watching the *Today* program.

The Suffolk County Court House in Pemberton Square is a very large gray building that's hard to see because it's halfway up the east flank of Beacon Hill and the new Government Center buildings shield it from what I still call Bowdoin Square and Scollay Square. I parked down in Bowdoin Square in front of the Saltonstall State Office Building and walked up the hill to the courthouse.

Jim Clancy had an Errol Flynn mustache, and it looked funny because his face was round and shiny and his light hair had receded hastily from his forehead. Sylvia and McDermott were there already, along with a guy who looked like Ricardo Montalban and one who looked like a Fed. McDermott introduced me. Ricardo turned out in fact to be Bobby Santos who might someday be public safety commissioner. The Fed turned out to be a man named Klaus from Treasury.

"We'll meet some people from Chelsea over there," McDermott said. "We've already filled Bobby in, and we're about to brief these gentlemen."

McDermott was wearing a green T-shirt today, with a pocket over the left breast, and gray corduroy pants, and sandals. His gun was stuck in his belt under the T-shirt, just above his belt buckle, and bulged like a prosthetic device. Klaus, in a Palm Beach suit, white broadcloth shirt and polka dot bow tie, looked at him like a virus. He spoke to Sylvia.

"What's Spenser's role in this?"

Sylvia said, "Why not ask him?"

"I'm asking you," Klaus said.

Sylvia looked at McDermott and raised his eyebrows. McDermott said, "Good heavens."

"Did I ever explain to you," Sylvia said to McDermott, "why faggots wear bow ties?"

I said to Klaus, "I'm the guy set it up. I'm the one knows the people and I'm the one that supervises the swap. I'm what you might call your key man."

Clancy said, "Go ahead, McDermott. Lay it out for us, we want to get the arrangements set."

McDermott lit a miserable-looking cigarette from the pack he kept in the pocket of his T-shirt.

"Well," he said, "me and Jackie was sitting around the squad room one day, thinking about crime and stuff, it was kind of a slow day, and here comes this key man here."

Klaus said, "For crissake, get on with it."

Santos said, "Rich."

McDermott said, "Yeah, yeah, okay, Bobby. I just don't want to go too fast for the G-man."

"Say it all, Rich," Santos said.

He did. The plan called for two vans, produce trucks, with Sylvia, McDermott, Santos, Linhares, Klaus and several Chelsea cops and two Staties from Clancy's staff to arrive in the area about five-thirty, park at a couple of unloading docks, one on one side and one on the other side of the restaurant, and await developments. When the time was right I'd signal by putting both hands in my hip pockets, and "Like locusts," McDermott said, "me and Jackie and J. Edgar over here will be on 'em."

Clancy opened a manila folder on his desk and handed around 8 x 10 glossy mug shots of King Powers. "That's Powers," Clancy said. "We have him on file."

"The two women," I said, "I'll have to describe." And I did. Klaus took notes, Sylvia cleaned his fingers with the small blade of a pocketknife. The others just sat and looked at me. When I got through, Klaus said, "Good descriptions, Spenser."

McDermott and Sylvia looked at each other. Tomorrow it would be good if they were in one truck and Klaus was in another.

Clancy said, "Okay, any questions."

Santos said, "Warrants?"

Clancy said, "That's in the works, we'll have them ready for tomorrow."

Santos said, "How about entrapment."

"What entrapment," Sylvia said. "We got a tip from an informant that an illegal gun sale was going down, we staked it out and we were lucky."

Clancy nodded. "It should be clean, all we're arranging is the stakeout. We had nothing to do with Spenser double-crossing them."

"One of my people's going to be there, Pam Shepard. You'll probably have to pick her up. If you do, keep her separate from the others and give her to me as soon as the others are taken away."

"Who in hell are you talking to, Spenser," Klaus said. "You sound like you're in charge of the operation."

McDermott said, "Operation, Jackie. That's what we're in, an operation."

Clancy said, "We agreed, Clyde. We trade the broad and her husband for Powers and the libbers."

"Clyde?" Sylvia said to McDermott.

"Clyde Klaus?" McDermott's face was beautiful with pleasure.

Klaus's face flushed slightly.

"Clyde Klaus." McDermott and Sylvia spoke in unison, their voices breaking on the very edge of a giggle.

Santos said, "You two clowns wanna knock off the horseshit. We got serious work to do here. Cruz got you detached to me on this thing, you know. You listen to what I tell you."

Sylvia and McDermott forced their faces into solemnity behind which the giggles still smirked.

"Anything else?" Clancy said. He turned his head in a half circle, covering all of us, one at a time. "Okay, let's go look at the site."

"I'll skip that one," I said. "I'll take a look at it later. But if any of the bad persons got it under what Klaus would call surveillance I don't want to be spotted with a group of strange, fuzzy-looking men."

"And if they see you looking it over on your own," Santos said, "they'll assume you're just careful. Like they are. Yeah. Good idea."

"You know the place?" Clancy said.

"Yeah."

"Okay, the Chelsea people are going to be under command of a lieutenant named Kaplan if you want to check on something over there."

I nodded. "Thanks, Clancy, nice to have met you gentlemen. See you tomorrow." I went out of Clancy's office. With the door ajar I reached back in with my right hand, gave it the thumbs-up gesture and said, "Good hunting, Clyde," and left. Behind me I could hear Sylvia and McDermott giggling again, now openly. Klaus said, "Listen," as I closed the door.

Outside I bought two hot dogs and a bottle of cream soda from a street vendor and ate sitting by the fountain in City Hall Plaza. A lot of women employed in the Government Center buildings were lunching also on the plaza and I ranked them in the order of general desirability. I was down to sixteenth when my lunch was finished and I had to go to work. I'd have ranked the top twenty-five in that time normally, but there was a three-way tie for seventh and I lost a great deal of time trying to resolve it.

Chelsea is a shabby town, beloved by its residents, across the Mystic River from Boston. There was a scatter of junk dealers, rag merchants and wholesale tire outlets, a large weedy open area where a huge fire had swallowed half the city, leaving what must be the world's largest vacant lot. On the northwest edge of the city where it abuts Everett is the New England Produce Center, one of two big market terminals on the fringes of Boston that funnel most of the food into the city. It was an ungainly place, next door to the Everett oil farm, but it sports a restaurant housed in an old railroad car. I pulled my car in by the restaurant and went in. It bothered me a little, as I sat at the counter and looked out at it, that my car seemed to integrate so aptly with the surroundings.

I had a piece of custard pie and a cup of black coffee and looked things over. It was a largely idle gesture. There was no way I could know where the swap would take place. There wasn't a hell of a lot for me to gain by surveying the scene. I had to depend on the buttons to show up, like they said they would when I put my hands in my hip pockets.

The restaurant wasn't very busy, more empty than full, and I glanced around to see if anyone was casing me. Or looked suspicious. No one was polishing a machine gun, no one was picking his teeth with a switchblade, no one was paying me any attention at all. I was used to it. I sometimes went days when people paid no attention to me at all. The bottom crust on my custard pie was soggy. I paid the bill and left.

I drove back into Boston through Everett and Charlestown. The elevated had been dismantled in Charlestown and City Square looked strangely naked and vulnerable without it. Like someone without his accustomed eyeglasses. They could have left it up and hung plants from it.

For reasons that have never been clear to me the midday traffic in Boston is as bad as the commuter traffic and it took me nearly thirty-five minutes to get to my apartment. Pam Shepard let me in looking neat but stir-crazy.

"I was just having a cup of soup," she said. "Want some?"

"I ate lunch," I said, "but I'll sit with you and have a cup of coffee while you eat. We're going to have to spend another night together."

"And?"

"And then I think we'll have it whipped. Then I think you can go home."

We sat at my counter and she had her tomato soup and I had a cup of instant coffee.

"Home," she said. "My god, that seems so far away."

"Homesick?"

"Oh, yes, very much. But . . . I don't know. I don't know about going home. I mean, what has changed since I left."

"I don't know. I guess you'll have to go home and find out.

Maybe nothing has changed. But tomorrow Rose and Jane are going to be in the jug and you can't sleep here forever. My restraint is not limitless."

She smiled. "It's kind of you to say so."

"After tomorrow we can talk about it. I won't kick you out."

"What happens tomorrow?"

"We do it," I said. "We go over to the Chelsea Market about six in the morning and we set up the gun sale and when it is what you might call consummated, the cops come with the net and you and Harv get another crack at it."

"Why do I have to go? I don't mean I won't, or shouldn't, but what good will I do?"

"You're kind of a hostage . . . Rose figures if you're implicated too, I won't double-cross them. She doesn't trust me, but she knows I'm looking out for you."

"You mean if she gets arrested, I'll get arrested too?"

"That seems her theory. I told her that didn't seem sisterly. She said something about the cause."

"Jesus Christ, maybe you are the only person I can depend on."

I shrugged.

26

IT WAS RAINING like hell and still dark when I woke up with a crick in my neck on the sofa in my living room. I shut off the alarm and dragged myself out of bed. It was quarter of five. I took a shower, and got dressed before I banged on my bedroom door, at five o'clock.

Pam Shepard said, "I'm awake."

She came out of the bedroom wearing my bathrobe and looking her age and went into the bathroom. I checked my gun. I stood in my front window and looked down at Marlborough Street and at the rain circles forming in the wet street. I thought about making coffee and decided we wouldn't have time and we could get some in the railroad car. I got out my red warm-up jacket that said LOWELL CHIEFS on it and put it on. I tried getting the gun off my hip while wearing it, and, if I left it unbuttoned, it wasn't bad. At five-twenty Pam Shepard came out of the bathroom with her hair combed and her make-up on and my robe still folded around her, and went back into my bedroom and shut the door. I took my car keys out of my hip pocket and put them in my coat pocket. I went to the window and looked at the rain some more. It always excited me when it rained. The wet streets seemed more promising than the dry ones, and the city was quieter. At five-thirty Pam Shepard came out of my bedroom wearing yellow slacks and a chocolate-colored blouse with long lapels. She put on a powder blue slicker and a wide-brimmed rain hat that matched and said, "I'm ready."

"The wardrobe for every occasion," I said. "I have the feeling you had Susan buy you a safari hat just in case you had to shoot tiger while you stayed here."

She smiled but there wasn't much oomph in it. She was scared.

"This is going to be a milk run," I said. "There will be more cops than fruit flies there. And me, I will be right with you."

We went down the front stairs and got in my car and it started and we were off.

"I know," she said. "I know it'll be all right. There's just been so much, and now this. Police and gangsters and it's early in the morning and raining and so much depends on this."

"You and me, babe," I said, "we'll be fine." I patted her leg. It was a gesture my father used to make. It combined, when he did it, affection and reassurance. It didn't seem to do a hell of a lot for Pam Shepard. At twelve minutes of six in the morning we pulled into the restaurant parking lot. It was daylight now, but a gray and dismal daylight, cold as hell, for summer, and the warm yellow of the lighted windows in the railroad car looked good. There were a lot of trucks and cars parked. The terminal does its work very early. I assumed that two of the trucks contained our side but there was no telling which ones.

Inside we sat in a booth and ordered two coffees and two English muffins. Pam didn't eat hers. At about two minutes past six King Powers came in wearing a trench coat and a plaid golf cap. Macey was with him in a London Fog, and outside in the entryway I could see Hawk in what looked like a white leather cape with a hood.

"Good morning, Kingo-babe," I said. "Care for a cup of java? English muffin? I think my date's not going to eat hers."

Powers sat down and looked at Pam Shepard. "This the buyer," he said.

"One of them. The ones with the bread haven't shown up yet."

"They fucking better show up," King said. Macey sat in the booth beside Powers.

"That's a most fetching hat, King," I said. "I remember my Aunt Bertha used to wear one very much like it on rainy days. Said you get your head wet you got the miseries."

Powers paid no attention to me. "I say fucking six o'clock I mean fucking six o'clock. I don't mean five after. You know what I'm saying."

Rose and Jane came into the restaurant.

"Speak of coincidence, King," I said. "There they are."

I gestured toward Rose and Jane and pointed outside. They turned and left. "Let us join them," I said, "outside where fewer people will stand around and listen to us."

Powers got up, Macey went right after him and Pam and I followed along. As we went out the door I looked closely at Hawk. It was a white leather cape. With a hood. Hawk said, "Pow'ful nice mawning, ain't it, boss."

I said, "Mind if I rub your head for luck?"

I could see Hawk's shoulders moving with silent laughter. He drifted along behind me. In the parking lot I said, "King, Macey, Hawk, Rose, Jane, Pam. There now, we're all introduced, let us get it done."

Powers said, "You got the money?"

Jane showed him a shopping bag she was carrying under her black rubber raincoat.

"Macey, take it to the truck and count it."

Rose said, "How do we know he won't run off with it?"

Powers said, "Jesus Christ, sister, what's wrong with you?"

Rose said, "We want to see the guns."

"They're in the back of the truck," Macey said. "We'll get in and you can look at the guns while I count the money. That way we don't waste time and we both are assured."

Powers said, "Good. You do that. I'm getting out of the fucking rain. Hawk, you and Macey help them load the pieces when Macey's satisfied."

Powers got up in the cab of a yellow Ryder Rental Truck and closed the door. Rose and Jane and Macey went to the back of the truck. Macey opened the door and the three of them climbed in. Hawk and I and Pam Shepard stood in the rain. In about one minute Rose leaned out of the back of the truck.

"Spenser," she said, "would you check this equipment for us?"

I said to Pam, "You stand right there. I'll be right back." Hawk was motionless beside her, leaning against the front fender of the truck. I went around back and climbed in. The guns were there. Still in the original cases. M2 carbines. I checked two or three. "Yeah," I said, "they're good. You can waste platoons of old men now."

Rose ignored me. "All right, Jane, bring the truck over here. Spenser, you said you'd help us load the truck."

"Yes, ma'am," I said. "Me and Hawk."

Macey took the shopping bag that said FILENE'S on it, jumped down and went around to where Powers sat in the cab. He handed the money in to Powers and came back to the tailgate. "What do you think, Spenser. This okay to make the swap."

We were to the side of and nearly behind the restaurant. "Sure," I said. "This looks fine. Nobody around. Nobody pays any attention anyway. They load and unload all day around here."

Macey nodded. Jane backed in a blue Ford Econoline van, parked it tail to tail with Powers' truck, got out and opened the back doors. I went back to the front of the truck where Pam and Hawk were standing. "Hawk," I said softly, "the cops are coming. This is a setup." Macey and Rose and Jane were conspiring to move one case of guns from the truck to the van. "Hawk," Macey yelled, "you and Spenser want to give us a hand." Hawk walked silently around the front of the truck behind the restaurant and disappeared. I put my hands in my hip pockets. "Stay right beside me," I said to Pam Shepard.

From a truck that said ROLLIE'S PRODUCE Sylvia and McDermott and two state cops emerged with shotguns.

Jane screamed, "Rose," and dropped her end of the crate. She fumbled in the pocket of her raincoat and came out with a gun. Sylvia chopped it out of her hand with the barrel of the shotgun and she doubled over, clutching her arm against her. Rose said, "Jane," and put her arms around her. Macey dodged around the end of the van and ran into the muzzle of Bobby Santos' service revolver, which Santos pressed firmly into Macey's neck. King Powers never moved. Klaus and three Chelsea cops came around the other side of the truck and opened the door. One of the Chelsea cops, a fat guy with a boozer's nose, reached in and yanked him out by the coat front. Powers said nothing and did nothing except look at me.

I said to King, "Peekaboo, I see you," nodded at Jackie Sylvia, took Pam Shepard's hand and walked away. At seven we were in a deli on Tremont Street eating hash and eggs and toasted bagels and cream cheese and looking at the rain on the Common across the street.

"Why did you warn that black man?" Pam Shepard said, putting cream cheese on her bagel. She had skipped the hash and eggs, which showed you what she knew about breakfasts. The waitress came and poured more coffee in both our cups.

"I don't know. I've known him a long time. He was a fighter when I was. We used to train together sometimes."

"But isn't he one of them? I mean isn't he the, what, the muscle man, the enforcer, for those people?"

"Yeah."

"Doesn't that make a difference? I mean you just let him go."

"I've known him a long time," I said.

27

IT WAS STILL RAINING when we drove back to my apartment to get Pam's things, and it was still raining when we set out at about eight-thirty for Hyannis. There's an FM station in Boston that plays jazz from six in the morning until eleven. I turned it on. Carmen McRae was singing "Skyliner." The rain had settled in and came steadily against the windshield as if it planned to stay a while. My roof leaked in one corner and dripped on the back seat.

Pam Shepard sat quietly and looked out the side window of the car. The Carmen McRae record was replaced by an album of Lee Wiley singing with Bobby Hackett's cornet and Joe Bushkin's piano. Sweet Bird of Youth. There wasn't much traffic on Route 3. Nobody much went to the Cape on a rainy midweek morning.

"When I was a little kid," I said, "I used to love to ride in the rain, in a car. It always seemed so self-contained, so private." There we were in the warm car with the music playing, and the rest of the world was out in the rain getting wet and shivering. "Still like it, in fact."

Pam Shepard kept looking out the side window. "Is it over, do you think?" she said.

"What?"

"Everything. The bank robbery, the trouble Harvey is in, the hiding out and being scared? The feeling so awful?"

"I think so," I said.

"What is going to happen to Harvey and me?"

"Depends, I guess. I think you and he can make it work better than it has worked."

"Why?"

"Love. There's love there in the relationship."

"Shit," she said.

"Not shit," I said. "Love doesn't solve everything and it isn't the only thing that's important, but it has a big head start on everything else. If there's love, then there's a place to begin."

"That's romantic goo," Pam Shepard said. "Believe me. Harvey's preached the gospel of love at me for nearly twenty years. It's crap. Believe me, I know."

"No, you don't know. You've had a bad experience, so you think it's the only experience. You're just as wrong as Harvey. It didn't work, doesn't mean it won't work. You're intelligent, and you've got guts. You can do therapy. Maybe you can get Harv to do it. Maybe when you've gotten through talking about yourself with someone intelligent you'll decide to roll Harv anyway. But it'll be for the right reasons, not because you think you're frigid, or he thinks you're frigid. And if you decide to roll Harv you'll have some alternatives beside screwing sweaty drunks in one-night cheap hotels, or living in a feminist commune with two cuckoos."

"Is it that ugly," she said.

"Of course it's that ugly. You don't screw people to prove things. You screw people because you like the screwing or the people or both. Preferably the last. Some people even refer to it as making love."

"I know," she said, "I know."

"And the two dimwits you took up with. They're theoreticians. They have nothing much to do with life. They have little connection with heartbeats and stomach aches and wet feet. They have connection with phallic power and patterns of dominance and blowing away old men in the service of things like that."

She stopped looking out the window and looked at me. "Why so angry," she said.

"I don't know exactly. Thoreau said something once about judging the cost of things in terms of how much life he had to expend to get it. You and Harv aren't getting your money's worth. Thrift, I guess. It violates my sense of thrift."

She laughed a little bit and shook her head. "My god, I like you," she said. "I like you very much."

"It was only a matter of time," I said.

She looked back out the window and we were quiet most of the rest of the drive down. I hadn't said it right. Maybe Suze could. Maybe nobody could. Maybe saying didn't have much effect anyway.

We got to the motel a little after ten and found Susan in the coffee shop drinking coffee and reading the *New York Times*.

"Was it okay," Susan said.

"Yeah, just the way it should have been."

"He warned one of them," Pam Shepard said. "And he got away."

Susan raised her eyebrows at me.

"Hawk," I said.

"Do you understand that," Pam Shepard said.

"Maybe," Susan said.

"I don't."

"And I'll bet he didn't give you a suitable explanation, did he?" Susan said.

"Hardly," Pam said.

"Everything else was good though?" Susan said.

I nodded.

"Are you going home, Pam?"

"I guess I am. I haven't really faced that, even driving down. But here I am, half a mile from my house. I guess I am going home."

"Good."

"I'm going to call Harv," I said. "How about I ask him to join us and we can talk about everything and maybe Suze can talk a little."

"Yes," she said. "I'm scared to see him again. I'd like to see him with you here and without the children."

I went back to the room and called Shepard and told him what had happened. It took him ten minutes to arrive. I met him in the lobby.

"Is Powers in jail?" he said.

I looked at my watch. "No, probably not. They've booked him by now, and his lawyer is there arranging bail and King's sitting around in the anteroom waiting to go home."

"Jesus Christ," Shepard said. "You mean he's going to be out loose knowing we set him up?"

"Life's hard sometimes," I said.

"But, for crissake, won't he come looking for us? You didn't tell me they'd let him out on bail. He'll be after us. He'll know we double-crossed him. He'll be coming."

"If I'd told you, you wouldn't have done it. He won't come after you."

"What the hell is wrong with them, letting him out on bail. You got no right to screw around with my life like that."

"He won't come after you, Shepard. Your wife's waiting for you in the coffee shop."

"Jesus, how is she?"

"She's fine."

"No, I mean, like what's her frame of mind? I mean, what's she been saying about me? Did she say she's going to come back?"

"She's in the coffee shop with my friend Susan Silverman. She wants to see you and she wants us to be there and what she's going to do is something you and she will decide. She's planning, right now, I think, to stay. Don't screw it up."

Shepard took a big inhale and let it out through his nose. We went into the coffee shop. Susan and Pam Shepard were sitting opposite each other in a booth. I slid in beside Susan. Shepard stood and looked down at Pam Shepard. She looked up at him and said, "Hello, Harv."

"Hello, Pam."

"Sit down, Harv," she said. He sat, beside her. "How have you been?" she said.

He nodded his head. He was looking at his hands, close together on the table before him.

"Kids okay?"

He nodded again. He put his right hand out and rested it on her back between the shoulder blades, the fingers spread. His eyes were watery and when he spoke his voice was very thick. "You coming back?"

She nodded. "For now," she said and there was strain now in her voice too.

"Forever," he said.

"For now, anyway," she said.

His hand was moving in a slow circle between her shoulder blades. His face was wet now. "Whatever you want," he said in his squeezed voice. "Whatever you want. I'll get you anything you want, we can start over and I'll be back up on top for you in a year. Anything. Anything you want."

"It's not up on top I want, Harvey." I felt like a voyeur. "It's, it's different. They think we need psychiatric help." She nodded toward me and Suze.

"What do they know about it, or us, or anything?"

"I won't stay if we don't get help, Harvey. We're not just unhappy. We're sick. We need to be cured."

"Who do we go to? I don't even know any shrinks."

"Susan will tell us," Pam said. "She knows about these things."

"If that's what will bring you back, that's what I'll do." His voice was easing a little, but the tears were still running down his face. He kept rubbing her back in the little circles. "Whatever you want."

I stood up. "You folks are going to make it. And while you are, I'm going to make a call."

They paid me very little heed and I left feeling about as useful as a faucet on a clock. Back in the room I called Clancy in the Suffolk County D.A.'s office.

"Spenser," I said when he came on. "Powers out of the calaboose yet?"

"Lemme check."

I listened to the vague sounds that a telephone makes on hold for maybe three minutes. Then Clancy came back on. "Yep."

"Dandy," I said.

"You knew he would be," Clancy said. "You know the score."

"Yeah, thanks." I hung up.

Back in the coffee shop Pam was saying, "It's too heavy. It's too heavy to carry the weight of being the center of everybody's life."

The waitress brought me another cup of coffee.

"Well, what are we supposed to do," Harv said. "Not love you. I tell the kids, knock it off on the love. It's too much for your mother? Is that what we do?"

Pam Shepard shook her head. "It's just . . . no of course, I want to be loved, but it's being the *only* thing you love, and the kids, being so central, feeling all that . . . I don't know . . . responsibility, maybe, I want to scream and run."

"Boy" — Harv shook his head — "I wish I had that problem, having somebody love me too much. I'd trade you in a goddamned second."

"No you wouldn't."

"Yeah, well, I wouldn't be taking off on you either. I don't even know where you been. You know where I been."

"And what you've been doing," she said. "You goddamned fool."

Harv looked at me. "You bastard, Spenser, you told her."

"I had to," I said.

"Well, I was doing it for you and the kids. I mean, what kind of man would I be if I let it all go down the freaking tube and you and the kids had shit? What kind of a man is that?"

"See," Pam said. "See, it's always me, always my responsibility. Everything you do is for me."

"Bullshit. I do what a man's supposed to do. There's nothing peculiar about a man looking out for the family. Dedicating his life to his family. That's not peculiar. That's right."

"Submerging your own ego to that extent is unusual," Susan said.

"Meaning what?" Shepard's voice had lost its strangled quality and had gotten tinny. He spoke too loudly for the room.

"Don't yell at Suze, Harv," I said.

"I'm not yelling, but, I mean, Christ, Spenser, she's telling me that dedication and self-sacrifice is a sign of being sick."

"No she's not, Harv. She's asking you to think why you can't do anything in your own interest. Why you have to perceive it in terms of self-sacrifice."

"I, I don't perceive . . . I mean I can do things I want to . . . for myself."

"Like what?" I said.

"Well, shit, I . . . Well, I want money too, and good things for the family . . . and . . . aw, bullshit. Whose side are you on in this?"

Pam Shepard put her face in her hands. "Oh god," she said. "Oh god, Jesus goddamned Christ," she said.

28

THE SHEPARDS went home after a while, uneasy, uncertain, but in the same car with the promise that Susan and I would join them for dinner that night. The rain stopped and the sun came out. Susan and I went down to Sea Street beach and swam and lay on the beach. I listened to the Sox play the Indians on a little red Panasonic portable that Susan had given me for my birthday. Susan read Erikson and the wind blew very gently off Nantucket Sound. I wondered when Powers would show up. Nothing much to do about that. When he showed he'd show. There was no way to prepare for it.

The Sox lost to Cleveland and a disc jockey came on and started to play "Fly Robin Fly."

I shut off the radio.

"You think they'll make it?" I said.

Susan shrugged. "He's not encouraging, is he?"

"No, but he loves her."

"I know." She paused. "Think we'll make it?"

"Yeah. We already have."

"Have we?"

"Yeah."

"That means that the status remains quo?"

"Nope."

"What does it mean?"

"Means I'm going to propose marriage."

Susan closed her book. She looked at me without saying anything. And she smiled. "Are you really?" she said.

"Yeah."

"Was that it?"

"I guess it was, would you care to marry me?"

She was quiet. The water on the sound was quiet. Easy swells looking green and deep rolled in quietly toward us and broke gently onto the beach.

Susan said, "I don't know."

"I was under a different impression," I said.

"So was I."

"I was under the impression that you wanted to marry me and were angry that I had not yet asked."

"That was the impression I was under too," Susan said.

"Songs unheard are sweeter far," I said.

"No, it's not that, availability makes you no less lovable. It's . . . I don't know. Isn't that amazing. I think I wanted the assurance of your asking more than I wanted the consummated fact."

"Consummation would hardly be a new treat for us," I said.

"You know what I mean," she said.

"Yeah, I do. How are you going to go about deciding whether you want to marry me or not?"

"I don't know. One way would be to have you threaten to leave. I wouldn't want to lose you."

"You won't lose me," I said.

"No, I don't think I will. That's one of the lovely qualities about you. I have the freedom, in a way, to vacillate. It's safe to be hesitant, if you understand that."

I nodded. "You also won't shake me," I said.

"I don't want to."

"And this isn't free-to-be-you-and-me stuff. This is free to be us, no sharesies. No dibs, like we used to say in the schoolyard."

"How dreadfully conventional of you." Susan smiled at me. "But I don't want to shake you and take up with another man. And I'm not hesitating because I want to experiment around. I've done that. I know what I need to know about that. Both of us do. I'm aware you might be difficult about sharing me with the guys at the singles bar."

"I'll say."

"There are things we have to think about though."

"Like what?"

"Where would we live?"

I was still lying flat and she was half sitting, propped up on her left elbow, her dark hair falling a little forward. Her interior energy almost tangible. "Ah-ha," I said.

She leaned over and kissed me on the mouth. "That's one of your great charms, you understand so quickly."

"You don't want to leave your house, your work."

"Or a town I've lived in nearly twenty years where I have friends, and patterns of life I care about."

"I don't belong out there, Suze," I said.

"Of course you don't. Look at you. You are the ultimate man, the ultimate adult in some ways, the great powerful protecting father. And yet you are the biggest goddamned kid I ever saw. You would have no business in the suburbs, in a Cape Cod house, cutting the lawn, having a swim at the club. I mean you once strangled a man to death, did you not?"

"Yeah, name was Phil. Never knew his other name, just Phil. I didn't like it."

"No, but you like the kind of work where that kind of thing comes up."

"I'm not sure that's childish."

"In the best sense it is. There's an element of play in it for you, a concern for means more than ends. It comes very close to worrying about honor."

"It often has to do with life and death, sweetie."

"Of course it does, but that only makes it a more significant game. My neighbors in Smithfield are more serious. They are dealing with success or failure. For most of them it's no fun."

"You've thought about me some," I said.

"You bet your ass I have. You're not going to give up your work, I'm not going to stop mine. I'm not going to move to Boston. You're not going to live in Smithfield."

"I might," I said. "We could work something out there, I think. No one's asking you to give up your work, or me to give up mine."

"No, I guess not. But it's the kind of thing we need to think on."

"So a firm I-don't-know is your final position on this?"

"I think so."

I put my hands up and pulled her down on top of me. "You impetuous bitch," I said. Her face pressed against my chest. It made her speech muffled.

"On the other hand," she mumbled, "I ain't never going to leave you."

"That's for sure," I said. "Let's go have dinner and consummate our friendship."

"Maybe," Susan said as we drove back to the motel, "we should consummate it before dinner."

"Better still," I said, "how about before and after dinner?"

"You're as young as you feel, lovey," Susan said.

29

WE RANG the bell at the Shepards' house at seven-thirty, me with a bottle of Hungarian red wine in a brown paper bag, and Hawk opened the door and pointed a Colt .357 Magnum at me.

"Do come in," he said.

We did. In the living room were King Powers and Powell, the stiff I had knocked in the pool, and Macey and the Shepards. The Shepards were sitting on the couch together with Powell standing by with his gun out, looking at them, hard as nails. Macey stood by the mantel with his slim-line briefcase and Powers was in a wing chair by the fireplace. Shepard's face was damp and he looked sick. Getting beaten up tends to take a lot of starch out of a person and Shepard looked like he was having trouble holding it together. His wife had no expression at all. It was as if she'd gone inside somewhere and was holding there, waiting.

"Where's the kids?" I said.

Hawk smiled. "They not here. Harv and the Mrs., I guess, thought they'd have a quiet time together, 'fore you come, so they shipped 'em off to neighbors for the night. That do make it cozier, I say."

Powers said, "Shut up, Hawk. You'd fuck around at your own funeral."

Hawk winked at me. "Mr. Powers a very grumpy man and I do believe I know who he grumpy at, babe."

"I figured I'd be seeing you, King," I said.

"You figured fucking right, too, smart guy. I got something for you, you son of a bitch. You think you can drop me into the bag like that and walk away, you don't know nothing about King Powers."

Macey said, "King, this is just more trouble. We don't need this. Why don't we just get going."

"Nope, first I burn this son of a bitch." Powers stood up. He was a paunchy man who looked like he'd once been thin, and his feet pointed out to the side like a duck's. "Hawk, take his gun away."

"On the wall, kid, you know the scene."

I turned and leaned against the wall and let him take the gun off my hip. He didn't have to search around. He knew right where it was. Probably smelled it. I stepped away from the wall. "How come you walk like a duck, King?" I said. Powers' red face deepened a bit. He stepped close to me and hit me in the face with his closed fist. I rocked back from the waist and didn't fall.

"Quack," I said. Powers hit me again, and cut my lip. It would be very fat in an hour. If I was around in an hour.

Susan said, "Hawk."

He shook his head at her. "Sit on the couch," he said.

Shepard said, "You gonna shoot us?" There wasn't much vitality in his voice.

"I'm fucking-A-well going to shoot this smart scumbag," Powers said. "Then maybe I'll like it so much I'll shoot the whole fucking bag of you. How's that sound to you, you fucking welcher."

"She's not in it," Shepard said, moving his head toward his wife. "Let her go. We got four kids. They never done anything to you."

Powers laughed with the inside of his upper lip showing. "But you did. You screwed me out of a lot of money, you gonna have to make that good to me."

"I'll make it good, with interest. Let her go."

"We'll talk about it, welcher. But I want to finish with this smart bastard first." He turned back to me and started to hit me again. I stepped inside and hit him hard in the side over the kidneys. His body was soft. He grunted with pain and buckled to his knees.

Macey brought out his little automatic and Powell turned his gun from the Shepards toward me.

Hawk said, "Hold it." There was no Amos and Andy mockery in it now.

Powers sat on the floor, his body twisted sideways, trying to ease the pain. His face red and the freckles looking pale against it.

"Kill him," he said. "Kill the fucker. Kill him, Hawk."

Susan said, "Hawk."

I kept my eyes on Hawk. Macey wouldn't have the stomach for it. He'd do it to save his ass, if he couldn't run. But not just standing there; that took something Macey didn't get in business school. Powell would do what he was told, but so far no one had told him. Hawk was the one. He stood as motionless as a tree. From the corner of my eye, I could see Shepard's hand go out and rest in the middle of his wife's back, between the shoulder blades.

Susan said again, "Hawk."

Powers, still sitting on the floor with his knees up and his white socks showing above his brown loafers, said, "Hawk, you bastard, do what you're told. Burn him. Blow him away. Right now. Kill him."

Hawk shook his head. "Naw."

Powers was on his knees now, struggling to his feet. He was so out of shape that just getting off the floor was hard for him. "No? Who the fuck you saying no to, nigger. Who pays your fucking ass? You do what you're told . . ."

Hawk's face widened into a bright smile. "Naw, I don't guess I am going to do what I'm told. I think I'm going to leave that up to you, boss."

Powell said, "I'll do it, Mr. Powers."

Hawk shook his head. "No, not you, Powell. You put the piece down and take a walk. You too, Macey. This gonna be King and Spenser here, one on one."

"Hawk, you gotta be out of your mind," Macey said.

"Hawk, what the fuck are you doing?" Powers said.

"Move it out, Macey," Hawk said. "You and Powell lay the pieces down on the coffee table and walk on away."

Powell said, "Hawk, for crissake . . ."

Hawk said, "Do it. Or you know I'll kill you."

Macey and Powell put the guns on the coffee table and walked toward the front door.

"What the fuck is happening here," Powers said. The color was down in his face now, and his voice was up an octave. "You don't take orders from this fucking coon, you take them from me."

"Racial invective," Hawk said to me.

"It's ugly," I said. "Ugly talk."

Powers said, "Macey. Call the cops when you get out, Macey. You hear me, you call the cops. They're going to kill me. This crazy nigger is trying to kill me."

Macey and Powell went out and closed the door. Powers' voice was high now. "Macey, goddamnit. Macey."

Hawk said, "They gone, King. Time for you to finish Spenser off, like you started to."

"I don't have a gun. You know that, Hawk. I never carry a piece. Lemme have Macey's."

"No guns, King. Just slap him around like you was doing before." Hawk put his .357 under his coat and leaned against the door with his arms folded and his glistening ebony face without expression. Powers, on his feet now, backed away two steps.

"Hey, wait up, now, hey, Hawk, you know I can't go on Spenser just me and him. I don't even know if you could. I mean that ain't fair, you know. I mean that ain't the way I work."

Hawk's face was blank. Harvey Shepard got off the couch and took a looping amateurish roundhouse right-hand haymaker at Powers. It connected up high on the side of Powers' head near his right ear and staggered him. It also probably broke a knuckle in Shepard's hand. It's a dumb way to hit someone but Harv didn't seem to mind. He plowed on toward Powers, catching him with a left hand on the face and knocking him down. Powers scrambled for the two guns on the coffee table as Shepard tried to kick him. I stepped between him and the guns and he lunged at my leg and bit me in the right calf.

I said, "Jesus Christ," and reached down and jerked him to his feet. He clawed at my face with both hands and I twisted him away from me and slammed him hard against the wall. He stayed that way for a moment, face against the wall, then turned slowly away from the wall, rolling on his left shoulder so that when he got through turning his back was against the wall. Shepard started toward him again and I put my hand out. "Enough," I said. Shepard kept coming and I had to take his shoulder and push him back. He strained against me.

From the couch Pam Shepard said, "Don't, Harvey." Shepard stopped straining and turned toward her. "Jesus," he said and went and sat on the couch beside her and put his arms awkwardly around her and she leaned against him, a little stiffly, but without resistance.

Susan got up and walked over and put her hands on Hawk's shoulders and, standing on her toes to reach, kissed him on the mouth.

"Why not, Hawk? I knew you wouldn't, but I don't know why."

Hawk shrugged. "Me and your old man there are a lot alike. I told you that already. There ain't all that many of us left, guys like old Spenser and me. He was gone there'd be one less. I'd have missed him. And I owed him one from this morning."

"You wouldn't have done it anyway," Susan said. "Even if he hadn't warned you about the police."

"Don't be too sure, honey. I done it lots of times before."

"Anyway, babe," Hawk said to me, "we even. Besides" — Hawk looked back at Susan and grinned — "Powers a foul-mouthed bastard, never did like a guy swore in front of ladies that way." He stepped across, dropped my gun on the table, picked up those belonging to Macey and Powell and walked out. "See y'all again," he said. And then he was gone.

I looked at Powers. "I think we got you on assault with intent to murder, King. It ain't gonna help iron out the trouble you're already in in Boston, is it."

"Fuck you," Powers said and let his legs go limp and slid onto the floor and sat still.

"Hawk was right, King," I said. "Nobody likes a garbage mouth."